I0598617

# LICENSE NOTE

# HOOKED ON EWE

AUTUMN IN WILD ROSE RIDGE

WILD ROSE ROSE RIDGE SERIES

DALYN WELLER

# THE LORD SEES THE HEART

> "Humans do not see what the Lord sees, for humans see what is visible, but the Lord sees the heart."
>
> 1 Samuel 16:7

> "So don't throw away your confidence, which has a great reward. For you need endurance, so that after you have done God's will, you may receive what was promised."
>
> Hebrews 10:35-36

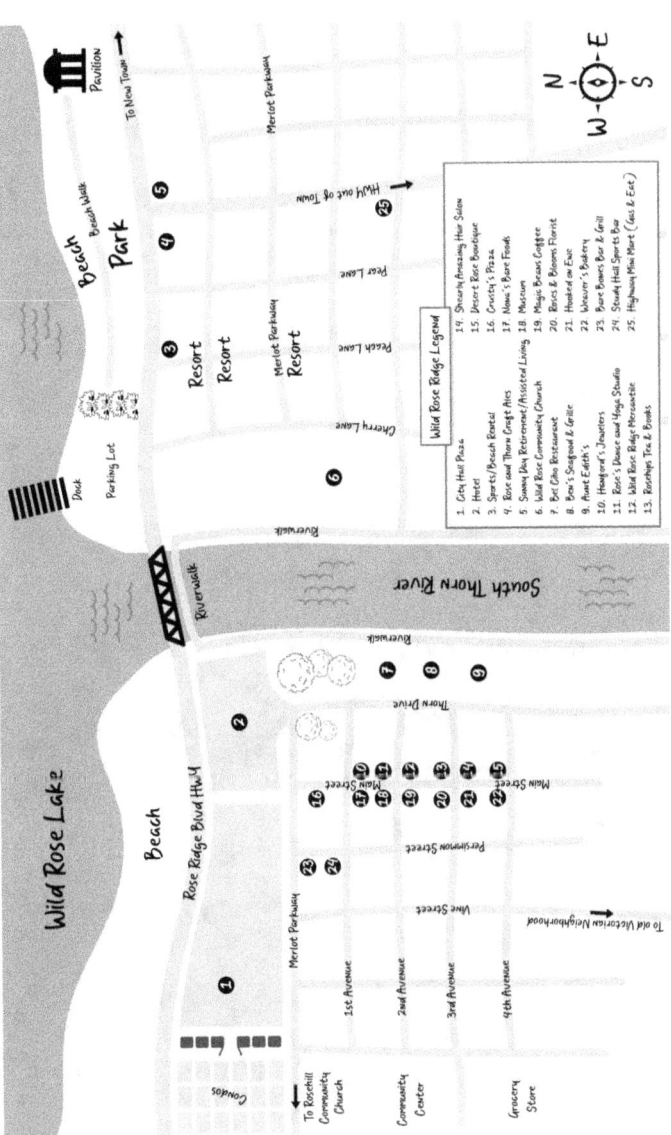

Wild Rose Lake

Beach

Wild Rose Ridge Hwy

Beach Park

Beach Walk

Pavilion

To New Town →

Dock

Parking Lot

Resort

Resort

Resort

South Thorn River

Riverwalk

Riverwalk

Riverwalk

Merlot Parkway

Pear Lane

Beach Lane

Cherry Lane

Merlot Parkway

Hwy out of Town →

Thorn Drive

Main Street

Main Street

Persimmon Street

Vine Street

To old Victorian Neighborhood →

Merlot Parkway

1st Avenue

2nd Avenue

3rd Avenue

4th Avenue

To Rosehill Community Church →

Condos

Community Center

Grocery Store

### Wild Rose Ridge Legend

1. City Hall Plaza
2. Hotel
3. Sports/Beach Rental
4. Root and Thorn Craft Ales
5. Sunny Day Retirement/Assisted Living
6. Wild Rose Community Church
7. Eat Cake Restaurant
8. Bea's Seafood & Grille
9. Aunt Edith's
10. Head of C's Jewelers
11. Rosie's Dance and Yoga Studio
12. Wild Rose Ridge Mercantile
13. Rooftops Tea & Books
14. Stitch in Time
15. Drive's Rose Boutique
16. Crusty's Pizza
17. Mona's Bare Foods
18. Museum
19. Strictly Amazing Hair Salon
20. Roses & Blooms Florist
21. Hooked on Ewe
22. Weaver's Bakery
23. Bone Bones Bar & Grill
24. Steady Hall Sports Bar
25. Highway Mini Mart (Gas & Eat)

N · E · S · W (compass)

*For my Wild Rose Ridge sisters,*
*We make a great team! Thanks for the prayers, the monthly*
*meetings, the brainstorming video chats, and the annual*
*retreat in the woods!*

*All my love,*
*Dalyn*

# CONTENTS

# SABOTAGE

*M*illie Rutherford loved her cozy little knitting shop. She and Walt—God rest him—had inherited it from her parents who had inherited it from Millie's grandparents. Walt had gone home to the Lord and Jarod, their only son, a confirmed bachelor had moved to Italy. Their absences left Millie without much to look forward to until her sister, Eugenia had asked her—make that begged her—to take her only daughter off her hands. Eugenia was at her wit's end with Olivia.

Olivia was pretty enough, and the girl was smart, but she was much too shy to make a match on her own. She needed a little help, and Millie was more than happy to assist. If she were being honest—which she mostly was—she'd admit that a little matchmaking would benefit her as much as the young couple.

Millie smiled at her daring plan. There were loads of eligible young men in Wild Rose Ridge, but she'd chosen the right man. She only needed to enlist the sisterhood's assistance.

Most unsuspecting folks supposed the knitting club to be

a band of old biddies, but if they knew what went on in the backroom of *Hooked On Ewe* during knitting club they'd give the ladies the respect due them. Millie's yarn shop had been the headquarters for the sisterhood since her grandmother's time and Lord willing, would still be operating long after Millie was resting in the boneyard alongside Walt.

If a person wanted to be dramatic about it—and Millie liked to be dramatic on occasion— they were a kind of shadow government. Mostly they were women who loved their town and the people in it, and if they sometimes had to manipulate circumstances for the greater good…so be it.

The bells on the front door jingled and the hinges squeaked. Millie flipped the switch on the electric kettle. Her ladies could solve world peace over a good pot of tea. She filled her mother's old Brown Betty pot with hot water to temper it, filled the sugar bowl, and pulled the milk from the mini refrigerator. Then she lit the electric fireplace to make the room cozy.

A cautious step sounded in the doorway. "Hello?" Ruthie Rosmund paused for a welcome.

"In the back, Ruthie," Millie called out. She poured milk into the porcelain creamer jug and set out the box of cookies she'd special ordered from Weaver's Bakery that morning.

Ruthie stood in the doorway with her head to one side. "Millie?" Her brows were pulled together in confusion. "Why are you here?"

"It's my store," Millie answered with some sauce.

Ruthie snorted. "Nobody said it wasn't." She came inside the back room, head whipping this way and that as she took in the tea things Millie had prepared. She sniffed the new tin of tea Millie bought from Rosehips Tea & Book Shop for her first meeting back. "Black raspberry?"

"We need all of our faculties." Millie lifted the lid from

the Brown Betty and measured loose tea from the tin. She filled an infuser, settled it into the opening of the pot, and poured boiling water from the kettle over it. "The tea will be ready in a bit."

The bells on the door sounded again and a chorus of female voices filled the shop. Millie winced when the door slammed.

"Smells good in here," Ellen Sutherland said in a cheery voice.

"Come in, girls." Millie stacked cookies on a pretty Wedgewood plate and set it next to the teapot.

"Millicent Rutherford, what on earth?" Diana dropped her bags in the doorway and Ellen, on her heels, bumped into her.

"Excuse me." Sniffed Margaret Walcott trying to see around her friends.

The front door opened again. "Hallooo," Shirley Shulte called.

Millie flashed her dentures to a roomful of her friends. Their penciled-on brows raised to their hairlines as they looked from Millie to one another.

"Come on girls, shut the door behind you and settle down." She needed to establish her control over this rowdy group right out of the gate. There was a lot at stake.

"Millie, what are you doing here?" Ellen poured herself a cup of tea and took the best seat.

Ruthie set her knitting bag next to Ellen and pulled out a mangled mess of yarn. She looked up, shrugged, and handed it to Ellen. "It's a baby blanket."

"I see you still haven't learned to knit, Ruthie."

"Millie, this is about your niece, isn't it?" Ruthie headed for the teapot.

"What's with the ladders?" Margaret asked.

Millie pushed the plate of cookies closer to Ruthie and offered her a teacup. "Still take two sugars?"

"Don't change the subject."

"Of course, it's about Olivia." Millie brushed past Ruthie and fixed her tea just so. She took a comfortable chair near the center of the room, ready to hijack the weekly meeting. She might as well get to the point. "Olivia's been here since May and hasn't gone on even one date."

"So, your sister did send Olivia here to find a husband." Margaret grinned. "I knew it."

Millie tested her brew, found it too hot, and blew on it. "I know I should have been around more and I'm sorry I haven't." She crossed her feet at the ankles. "I will be from now on."

Ruthie sent her a sympathetic look. "You were grieving your Walt. We understand, dear."

Diana came round and squeezed Millie's shoulder. "We guessed that Eugenia wanted help settling Olivia with a husband. What's the holdup?"

Millie settled her teacup on her knee. "Olivia doesn't even try. She's oblivious to men."

"There are lots of girls these days who wait too long and miss out," Ellen observed this with a note of disapproval.

Millie shook her head. "It's not that. The girl doesn't try. She hides her attributes behind baggy clothes and thick glasses. Eugenia wanted grandbabies yesterday, so she conjured up some story about me needing Olivia's help here for the tourist season and trusted me to help."

"Does Olivia know you're recruiting the Meddling Mamas to fix her love life?" Ellen kept her eyes on the needles and yarn tangled in her lap.

"She doesn't suspect a thing. She believes we're just a knitting club. She's asked to join twice but I've put her off."

Millie nibbled the edge of a cookie. "The thing is, Olivia is naive and sweet, but she's an old soul. She loves teaching her weekly knitting class, puttering in my garden, and guess what? She's gone and joined the Birding Betties."

"But they're all old ladies." Diana paused the teacup she was lifting to her lips. "There isn't one under seventy-five."

"Well, there is now." Millie rolled her eyes.

"Do you have some hapless man in mind, then?" Ruthie waggled her eyebrows.

"I do, but I need your help." Millie pointed a finger to the nearest ladder. "We're going to sabotage the shop as soon as we finish our tea." She sent a big smile around the room. It was good to be back.

An hour later she was climbing down from a ladder with Shirley's hands planted on her rear end to keep her from falling.

"You're acting crazy, Millie."

Millie presented her with a handful of batteries. "Only one more smoke alarm to go." She turned to Diana. "Were you able to remove the cover plates from the light switches on that wall?"

"Yes, and Ruthie's got the extension cord plugged in with all the extra fans and the espresso machine. If that's not a fire hazard I don't know what is." She waved a hand toward the corner of the room with a worried look.

"Good."

"Now will you tell us what this is about?" Ellen lugged the fire extinguisher she'd taken off the wall to the opposite side of the room.

Diana took it from her, crouching and nearly dropping it on her foot. The gray slacks she wore made her resemble a roly-poly bug poking her big, round bottom up while she shoved the metal container in the corner of the closet to hide it underneath a bag of wool.

"I found out from Chief Vick's wife that the fire department is conducting their safety inspections. They'll be on Main Street this week and on this side of the street tomorrow."

She leaned back and closed her eyes. "Now picture that handsome Simms boy in his uniform...how could Olivia resist?"

Understanding dawned on the faces around her, eyes began to glitter as mouths pulled up into smiles.

Millie brushed a clump of damp hair from her forehead. "So you see, we have to fail."

With a knowing look, Ruthie collapsed on the small sofa. "Aren't you a crafty fox? You need a reason for Wyatt Simms to return to the shop."

"Exactly. He'll have to cite us, maybe even fine us." She clapped her hands in glee, scheming was fun. "Wyatt has to return for another inspection after finding all the broken fire codes."

"Wyatt Simms, the firefighter in line to co-inherit Quail Hollow Vineyards?" Diana looked impressed. "A good choice."

"He's single, handsome, and he's kind." Millie climbed up the ladder to retrieve the batteries from another smoke detector.

Diana grinned. "And someday he'll be rich."

"He'd never meet our lovely Olivia if he didn't have to come to Hooked On Ewe. I've done a bit of spying, and I'm told he's an extremely popular young man. His large friend group hangs out at the Rose & Thorn Craft Ale House."

Ruthie frowned. "Olivia would never go there."

"No, but now that she's out of the shadow of her mother,

she's free to be herself. My sister tends to be a bit overbearing. Olivia will blossom in Wild Rose."

"Are you sure it's enough to merely allow Wyatt and Olivia to meet?" Ruthie was sharp. She was a pro matchmaker. After all, hadn't she gotten her difficult granddaughter Stormy married off to that handsome, rich cowboy? If the rumors were to be believed, it hadn't been an easy match to make. But Stormy was difficult while Olivia was only shy.

"He'll notice how pretty Olivia is on the first visit. When he has to come back after we fail the inspection, I'll make sure Olivia is the only one here."

"So, you plan to throw them together and hope for the best?" Diana said in a tone that stung. "And this started out so promising..."

"Do you have a better idea?" Millie challenged.

"We'll think of something, Millie dear." She smiled in a way that always made Millie shiver just a little. "We always do."

# 1

## CITATIONS AND FINES

*O*livia Lewis didn't have much going for her. By thirty, she found it more practical to lower her expectations of life rather than live in continual disappointment.

Until she came to Wild Rose Ridge. Now she wanted more.

While other women her age were busy with careers, babies, social media, and iced coffee, Olivia spent her days knitting and birdwatching. It was good to have hobbies, right? Romance novels were more comfortable than real-life romance, so she kept her Wild Rose Ridge library card handy. Everyone wanted to be loved, right? Maybe someday...

You never knew who you might meet in a tourist town. Of course, the yarn shop wasn't exactly a man magnet. Still, the Ridge provided a change of scenery, and she was overdue for a new start.

Working for Aunt Millie at Hooked On Ewe as the shop manager and knitting teacher was a dream come true. She probably shouldn't keep asking the Lord for more. Her stifling job under the head librarian, grumpy Della Potts, in

Kingston taught her to appreciate the sunshine on the Ridge and Millie's cheery company.

A knock on the window startled her, but she recovered her seat on the front counter stool.

Stella Montford poked her head in the door. "You're coming to the meeting, aren't you, dear?"

"I'm bringing the cookies from Weavers," Olivia said.

"Make sure you bring some Snickerdoodles." Stella closed the door, making the bells tied on the knob jingle.

Wiping crumbs from her lap, Olivia tidied away the rest of her sandwich. She shoved the half-eaten bag of chips on top of her Birding Betty notebook underneath the front counter. She tossed the last morsel of cheese to Morris, Millie's shop cat. He ignored the bite of cheddar.

"Beggars can't be choosers, kitty."

Morris meowed, twitched his tail, and gave her a disdainful eyeballing before he jumped off the counter and sauntered to the back of the yarn shop. The last time she'd offended Morris, he'd left a nasty surprise in her shoe. Rummaging under the counter, she found a half-eaten pepperoni stick. She chased after the cat, holding the treat out as a peace offering.

Morris sniffed it, flicked his ear, and bit gingerly, taking the beef stick between his sharp teeth.

"Whew. Disaster averted." With the cat satisfied, she could finish going through the online rental ads. Affordable rentals in this town were as rare as hen's teeth.

Olivia glanced over to the corner. She should send off the bags of fleece Millie purchased from a local sheep farm to be processed into yarn, but the view through the picture window distracted her. Late August, she was impressed with a show of burgundy, amber, and gold leaves that took her breath away. Kingston was all evergreens and misty-moist days. Fall on the Ridge had been a happy surprise.

But if she wanted a place of her own, she'd better keep scouring the rentals. A farm would be dreamy, but she'd settle for almost anything. Millie's house was small, and Olivia suspected she'd become used to living alone.

Olivia opened a search on her phone app for rentals in the area, but something outside the window caught her eye. She leaned back to catch the view as two good-looking fire-fighters in dark blue uniforms walked along Main. They must be on official business. Olivia removed her glasses and wiped smudges off the lenses with her shirt. She chuckled at the swiveling female heads following the Firefighter's progress down the street. She'd admit they were worth looking at.

The back door slammed, sending a startled Morris flying to land on a shelving unit filled with pink and blue calico print fabrics. The cat lost balance and stacked shelves of green florals scattered, piles of cottons, felts, and flannels toppled. Morris hopped to the next shelf before turning to hiss at Millie.

Millie shook her finger at the cat and turned away. "Liv, I've got to run. See you later."

Millie had been dodgy about why she needed to be absent from her shop today, but if it stayed quiet, Olivia hoped to catch her up on her notebook so it didn't bother her. One of her new friends in the Birding Betties club reported seeing a Breasted Warbler. Olivia wanted to jot down the location so she could hike out with binoculars on her next day off.

The shop's front door banged open, and a boisterous group of women spilled inside. The Ridge was a popular wedding destination because of the wineries—over forty of them—and the young, pretty girls appeared to be part of a bridal party. A blonde with smeared mascara focused on Millie. "Is this a knitting shop?"

Aunt Millie frowned, put out.

"We're on a wine tour for Mandy's bridal shower and thought it would be a hoot to learn to knit or sew," a brunette said around a wet belch.

They all giggled at the burp, especially the brunette.

"Granny hobbies are all the rage," said the young woman Olivia presumed to be Mandy. She wore an "I'm the Bride" sash, and her glassy eyes proved she was celebrating something.

"Come back on Thursday evening, girls." Aunt Millie gestured toward Olivia. "My niece teaches a knitting class; the bride's first week is free." She hurried them out of the shop.

Turning to Olivia, she narrowed her eyes appraisingly. "Perhaps you could put on a bit of lippy?" Millie pointed to her lips. "I keep a hairbrush in a basket underneath the vanity in the backroom."

"Thank you?" Olivia cocked her head, waiting for an explanation but got a big fat nothing besides the back door slamming shut.

Olivia was self-aware and a lack of style had been some-thing she always struggled with. Clothes and makeup didn't come easily. She walked to the back of the shop where Uncle Walt had installed a little jewel box of a bathroom next to the kitchenette and flipped on the bathroom light. A glance at her saggy faded, floral blouse reminded her to at least make an effort at work for Millie's sake if not her own.

Olivia got stuck on the *how* part of how to make a change.

She flipped off the light and went to the cozy kitchen, done in blue and white. She filled the electric kettle for tea, retrieved a champagne-colored scatter cushion from the floor, and tossed it on the velvet sofa in the snug sitting room. Millie's knitting club met in this room every week but, for some reason, wouldn't allow Olivia to join. That stung a bit. She scanned the room for something to wear, a sweater left behind or…yes, there, on the back of the sofa. Someone abandoned a cardigan. It was a bit ragged, but as she'd reminded Morris earlier, beggars couldn't be choosers.

Slipping her arms in the sleeves, she could almost hear Mom's opinion of the hand-knit sweater.

If Eugenia Lewis had her way, Olivia would be married and producing grandchildren—half a dozen or so by now. Mom often said hurtful things. "We wanted a houseful, but it wasn't meant to be." She'd skewer Dad with a look meant to blame him. "We'd have been much happier with more children in the house, and if Olivia had siblings, she might not have turned out so—" She would pause as if she couldn't think of the word.

"Mousy," Mom would say as if the thought had just occurred. But she'd said it too often for that to be true.

Olivia's heart still carried the bruise.

Then there was the not-so-small matter of Mom's behavior. She passed out Olivia's cell number like a store coupon and Olivia the bargain. Once, they'd been stopped for speeding, and Mom asked the policeman if he was single.

Olivia pushed her glasses up. Mom only wanted to keep up with her friends in granny bragging rights, but Olivia had disappointed her, plain and simple. It caused friction between them, so when Millie called Olivia to say she needed help in her shop, Olivia packed her Bug and drove her to the Ridge before the line went dead.

That could be an exaggeration, but only by a smidge.

She made a small pot of tea and took it to the front of the

shop. Sipping tea and working on her birding notebook between customers wasn't a bad way to spend her workday.

The bells on the front door of the shop jangled, snapping Olivia out of her thoughts. She froze as the two firefighters with iPads and notebooks under their arms walked inside. The older man nodded to Olivia and offered her a tired smile.

"Hello, I'm Lieutenant Moore, and this is Firefighter Simms. We're tasked with completing the fire code inspections for the buildings along Main Street." He spoke the words by rote, memorized hours ago, no doubt.

The inevitable happened. Olivia's cheeks burned, and her throat tightened. "Inspections?" She wouldn't wish she could disappear into the carpet fibers right now if she were more confident. The younger man leaned forward with his hand out and gave Olivia a smile that made her heart puddle into her sensible shoes. No wonder women rubbernecked past them.

"Wyatt Simms. I don't think we've met before." He cocked his head in a way that made the words a question.

Her brain clouded, and sweat began to tickle her scalp. Blast her shyness. It ruined her life.

Wyatt's eyes captured and held hers. It would be rude to turn away, so she did her best to smile past the discomfort. "No, I'm sure we haven't." She stopped herself from saying, *I'd remember if we had.*

"We'll try to make this brief. I'm sure you have other things to do." Lieutenant Moore consulted his iPad.

"Can I get you some tea?" Olivia asked in a hoarse voice.

Lieutenant Moore shook his head. "Can we get straight to the inspection, miss…?" He lifted a questioning brow.

Oh. She hadn't even introduced herself. "Olivia Lewis."

Wyatt Simms stepped in front of Lieutenant Moore with a

confident grin. "Well, Olivia, how about we check out the smoke detectors first?"

An hour later, both men were shaking their heads, and no one was smiling anymore.

"I don't understand how your aunt can run the store with so many fire code violations." Lieutenant Moore swiped his iPad screen with his eyebrows crashing together. "Millicent Rutherford has never failed an inspection before. She's never even had so much as one code violation." He gave Olivia a cool once-over.

Did he think it was Olivia's fault? Why did Aunt Millie have to leave her alone today of all days?

"How did the cover plates for the light switches all go missing?" Firefighter Simms probed with a gentle tone.

"I...I honestly don't have any idea. They were here yesterday. I'm sure they were here."

"Every single smoke detector is missing the batteries. Don't you find that odd?" The Lieutenant frowned. "Because I certainly do."

Olivia lifted her blouse away from her sticky skin, regretting the borrowed cardigan.

Wyatt Simms set his iPad down and focused on Olivia with kind, gray eyes. "Is it possible someone stole them?"

"Or forgotten to replace them," The Lieutenant said dryly.

Olivia's tongue stuck to the roof of her mouth. "I...well, I can't see how...but...the kitting club. I mean, they meet in the back room, but..." She choked on tears. "I don't know."

Wyatt Simms laid a gentle hand over hers. She refrained from jerking away. His skin touching hers tasered like a lightning strike. She peered up to find a sympathetic smile that threatened what little control she had over her emotions. She snuck a peek at his sun-kissed face, nose dusted with freckles and smooth jaw.

He caught her looking and smiled at her with his pearly and perfect teeth. "Olivia, please give this list to your employer…er, aunt."

Olivia found she couldn't turn away from Wyatt's gorgeous mouth. Who was born with a smile like that?

Wyatt handed her a list. "These are the things she'll have to fix before Hooked On Ewe passes inspection."

Lieutenant Moore shoved a fistful of papers her way. "These are citations and the accompanying fines for failure to comply with fire codes." His mouth went grim. "This place is a hazard."

"A hazard?"

"That's right. Looks like there's work to do before this place is up to code. Better get on it so we don't have to shut you down."

Olivia put a hand to her heart and in the other hand, she clutched proof of her failure as Millie's new shop manager.

## 2

## SHUT DOWN

*CW*yatt Simms squirmed in his sticky uniform shirt outside of Hooked On Ewe. Moore was in a mood. "Did you have to be so rude?"

Moore glared.

"And that stack of fines…I understand citations for fire code violations, but…"

"Watch and learn, Rookie."

"Yeah. Sure, Lieutenant." There was no point in arguing.

Wyatt glanced over his shoulder at the yarn store. He'd taken a sneaky peek at Olivia's ring finger. It was bare, but she might have a boyfriend. He checked the buttons of his uniform shirt and ran a hand through his hair. There was only one way to find out.

"My shift was over two hours ago. Let's get back to the station." Moore's crew had spent the whole night on a brush fire off the highway, and he was on overtime.

Wyatt was sympathetic. Nobody wanted to do building inspections, especially in uniform on a sunny day. He turned to Moore. "I forgot something, I'll meet you back at the rig."

Moore gave him a dirty look but lumbered toward their engine.

Wyatt backtracked a few feet to the door of Hooked On Ewe and slipped inside. He scratched the orange tabby draped over the counter and gave Olivia a friendly smile. She frowned.

"Was there something else?" The slight tremor in her voice killed him.

Their eyes met over the counter. Hers big and brown, reminding him of a wounded deer he'd found once in the forest.

"I wanted to apologize for my coworker. He was up all night fighting a structure fire." He shrugged. "But I guess that's no excuse."

Olivia sank her teeth into her bottom lip, hands rattling the stack of fines. Moore could be intimidating when he was running on fumes.

Wyatt pointed to the smoke detectors. "It won't take much to get up to code. I can come back later and help you."

Olivia's eyes widened, and her cheeks flushed in a way that only made her prettier. Her hands flew to a delicate gold cross at her throat. She wore an outfit his grandmother wouldn't be caught dead in, but she was still gorgeous.

"Thank you, but I'll have to speak with my aunt," she said. "I'm not sure how she wants me to handle this." She held up the paperwork. "These."

He stepped nearer and caught a whiff of lemons. Everything about this woman was fresh—nothing like the trying-too-hard women who trolled the firefighters like dedicated fishers. Wyatt avoided their hooks, but the occasional wave of loneliness took him by surprise.

He'd like to have a family someday. If he could have the kind of relationship his parents had, he'd be a happy man.

Wyatt leaned over and scratched behind the cat's ears to give himself time to come up with something brilliant to say to this intriguing woman. "So, your aunt's Millicent Rutherford?" Genius.

Olivia nodded and dropped her eyes to the stack of citations. Thank goodness because it was hard to think straight with her thick lashes sweeping her cheeks behind black-framed glasses. "I would have remembered if we'd met." He scratched his chin.

"I only moved here in May." She glanced at the door as if looking for an escape. Most women loved a uniform, but she was as nervous as a rabbit facing a fox. "To help my aunt run the shop."

"Where did you move from?" Did she think he was asking official questions? The way she started chowing down her fingernail made him wonder.

"I'm… I'm from Kingston."

"Went fishing with my dad and brother there once." He shoved his hands deep in his pockets. "Great fishing." He nodded like he knew even though he'd only gone the one time.

She shrugged one shoulder. "It's always rainy there."

Wyatt's charm wasn't working on Olivia. He wanted to make her smile, but he didn't have much time with Moore waiting on him. He flashed her an all-teeth smile. "Would you like to have dinner with me?"

Olivia's eyelashes flew up, and her eyes doubled in size. "Now?"

"No."

"Oh."

"I'd love to, but I'm on shift until tomorrow morning." He held his breath.

Olivia pulled a pair of knitting needles out from underneath the counter, and her hands went to town. She gnawed her lip and avoided eye contact.

"How about this week sometime?"

It seemed like forever before the knitting needles stopped clacking, but finally, Olivia lifted her face. "Thank you, but no. I... I'm busy."

Wyatt couldn't help it if his mouth itched to smile despite the damage to his ego. "Busy, huh?" He tickled under the cat's chin, and the tabby began to purr. "You're always busy? Or maybe you have a boyfriend? I guess I'd be surprised if someone like you didn't."

Olivia's mouth dropped open. She peered at him from under those impossible lashes. "Someone like me?"

"Someone so gorgeous." He blurted the words before his courage failed him. He was used to women on the prowl for a man in uniform. He wasn't used to having to try so hard.

Olivia's throat and face turned red. The girls who hung around the Rose & Thorn didn't blush. They were party girls who left him cold. He wasn't interested in shallow relationships, but this woman...she was different.

Olivia's knitting needles started clicking away again. He grinned at her.

The door swung open, and Olivia's knitting clattered to the floor.

Millicent Rutherford breezed in all smiles. "Well, if it isn't Wyatt Simms. My, don't you look good in that fireman's uniform." Millie elbowed her way past him to nod at Olivia. "Doesn't he look good enough to eat, Liv?"

Poor Olivia. The color drained from her cheeks, and she made a little choking sound.

Wyatt grinned and winked at Millie. Every guy raised on the Ridge knew the Meddling Mamas. His father called them the Menacing Mothers. Fondly, of course.

Olivia bent to scoop up her project.

"I was just asking Olivia if she'd like to have dinner with me tomorrow night."

Her needles clicked with a fury.

Millie's gaze traveled between Wyatt and Olivia with a crafty glint. "Where are you two going? El Cibo has an excellent cheese plate starter."

Olivia gulped. "I… I'm not…that is, I'm not hungry… most nights," she finished lamely.

Millie made frantic gestures she thought Wyatt couldn't see.

He gave the ladies a tight smile. "No worries. I'll be seeing you next week for another inspection." Asking Olivia out had been a bad idea.

Millie put a hand to her pillowy bosom. "Another inspection? I thought you finished your inspections on this street today." Something sly lurked in the back of her eyes.

Setting her knitting aside, Olivia held out the stack of citations Moore had written out.

Millicent's mouth bunched up as she flipped through the stack.

Olivia's color was higher than ever. Wyatt was tempted to offer his help again but decided against it. "I'd better be on my way." Moore would be fuming by now if he wasn't already asleep in the back of the rig.

"Wait, please." Millicent followed him outside, snagging his arm and holding him tight. "Sorry," she murmured into his shoulder, steering him a few doors down. "I apologize for my niece. It's not that she isn't interested. It's more that she's just sort of…"

"Shy," Wyatt supplied.

"Yes. Well." She let go of his arm and squared up with him.

He took a step back.

"Are you interested in getting to know Liv?" She crossed her arms over the shelf that was her bosom.

Had he ever been in a more awkward situation? He glanced down the sidewalk, hoping to see Moore storming back, asking what he thought he was up to, leaving him to wait so long.

"Start by being her friend." Millicent gave his sleeve a gentle tug. "I have an idea."

He readied to make his escape at a dead run, but the image of a pair of warm, beautiful brown eyes kept his feet planted.

"Join Olivia's knitting class on Thursday evenings. Get to know her; let her get to know you."

"Knitting class?" Was Millie serious?

"You'll have a chance to see the real Olivia. She keeps to herself."

"You think she might be interested if she has a chance to know me?" He squinted at her. It didn't sound unreasonable.

Millie's head bobbed, both chins quivering in excitement. "What's not to like? Shall I put your name on the roster then?"

Wyatt sucked in a breath and let it propel his answer. "I guess."

"Class starts at six, don't be late." She hurried away like she was afraid he'd change his mind.

He probably should. Then, he had an idea of his own. A litmus test of sorts. He hollered to Millicent's back. "Can I bring Steve?"

She stopped and turned around. "Is your friend looking for romance too?"

Wyatt chuckled. "Steve's my dog."

"In that case, I don't see why not." She smiled in a way that made him take another look.

Yep, this old bird was a crafty one.

Her smile dropped away. "As long as Steve doesn't upset Morris." She shook a finger.

"Morris?"

*ednesday night, Wyatt allowed his best friend Joey Tanner to talk him into dinner at the Rose & Thorn, but he'd rather be on a date with a pretty knitter. The single guys in the department hung out here when they weren't on shift, and the place was crowded as usual. Wyatt and his friends held a permanent claim on a table outside with string lighting and a firepit.

Joey was nowhere to be seen yet, but Wyatt ordered anyway and headed to their table with his tower of nachos. He waved to Stormy and Dawson McClure, local cattle ranchers. They must be enjoying a rare date night since the birth of their baby. Wyatt couldn't remember if it was a boy or a girl. Either way, he'd bet Ruthie Rosmund was more than happy to babysit her grandchild.

Wyatt had gone to school with Stormy and, like most guys in their class, had suffered a regrettable crush on her. She'd stomped him under her cowboy boot along with the others. The tough-looking cowboy she'd married must be more resilient than the Wild Rose Ridge boys.

The server brought the raspberry ale Wyatt had ordered, and just as he tipped her, Joey lurched over. Wyatt sighed when he spotted Joey's entourage behind him. Wyatt would need a new best friend if he didn't grow up or at least sober up. Lately, he invited the firehouse groupies to every meetup.

Christine Jackson crooked her finger at Wyatt by way of greeting. He wasn't a jerk, so he returned a half-hearted nod. Joey plunked down, swung his boots onto the table, and guzzled Wyatt's ale.

Wyatt gave Joey the stink eye, moved his nachos aside, and noted the nearly empty glass in Christine's hand. Experience taught him that she got pretty handsy after a few drinks. She'd skinned on a dress that didn't leave much to the imagination, and the bright lipstick on her mouth matched the greasy smears on her glass.

"Wyatt." She said his name as if he were her favorite drink.

He ignored her. She'd dated Joey last summer until they broke up over a medic on B shift. It seemed any guy in a uniform would do, and she appeared determined to get her claws into Wyatt next. He started a conversation with a friend at the next table but kept tabs on the foolishness from the corner of his eye.

Christine wobbled a bit on her high heels as she scanned the tables. Her friends crowded the bench, taking over the table.

"Fishing, Chris?" Joey's smile was thin. He was still angry at her for cheating on him.

"Very funny."

Wyatt leaned toward her. "Who are your friends?" He might as well know their names since they were scarfing his nachos.

"Angie and Trish, meet Wyatt Simms," Christine purred.

Trish's eyes roved over him. "Are you a firefighter too? You look like one."

"All those muscles," Angie said in a husky tone.

Trish scooted closer to him.

Wyatt scooted away.

"Hmmm…" Trish traced his bicep.

He flinched and moved out of her reach.

Trish's blouse slipped open, revealing too much, and her smile told him she knew it. He looked away.

Angie wore a top that bared her midriff and a skirt so short half the guys here would be waiting for her to drop something. Wyatt gathered his keys and stuffed them into his front pocket.

"Hey!" Hector Valdez, walking beside Jimmy Bellman, came their way carrying pitchers of foamy ale and steaming plates of loaded potato skins.

The seductive allure of bacon provoked Wyatt's hunger pangs. He'd happily devour the potatoes since his nachos were long gone, but he wasn't sticking around for tonight's floozy fest. Usually, he let the flirting slide, but he was in no mood tonight. He kept picturing big brown eyes in a sweet, blushing face.

Thursday night knitting class couldn't come fast enough.

# 3

## KNITTING CLASS

$O$livia hoped knitting class would be a distraction from two things. The first was the long list of fire code violations the firefighters had cited Hooked On Ewe for, and the second was the friendly firefighter Wyatt Simms with his smiling gray eyes. He had preoccupied her thoughts thoroughly. Outside of novels, it was rare to meet a man like Wyatt. He was kind and heart-meltingly handsome, which was too bad for her since most men found her dull and attractive men never thought of her at all.

Yet, to Olivia's disbelief, Wyatt was strolling inside the shop with his hair slicked back for her knitting class.

"Okay, Lord, what are You up to now?"

$W$yatt pep-talked himself from his truck, through the door of Hooked On Ewe, past the racks of sewing supplies and shelves of fabric, yarn, and more yarn. He spotted Olivia in the back of the store through a side door where the old ladies pretended to knit. At least that's what his mother said. Grandma wouldn't admit to anything.

He patted his leg so Steve would follow him inside.

Olivia paused in the middle of arranging chairs and stared.

What now? He hadn't thought past getting here.

A tug on Steve's leash jolted Wyatt out of his stupor. Olivia was probably wondering why he'd brought his dog with him. Steve made a beeline for her. Her guarded expression melted away as she knelt to let the black lab sniff her. The smile that split her face stopped Wyatt's heart. Good old Steve.

"I always wanted a dog." The peachy skin of Olivia's face glowed when she turned those soft brown eyes on Wyatt. "What's his name?" She bent down, and Steve took full advantage of her, licking her face while she rubbed his ears like they were old friends.

So, his dog was the way around Olivia's shyness. "That's Steve, and I'm sorry about his manners." Not really, Steve was doing a stellar job of thawing her out. "He's friendly, as you can see."

He glanced around the back room, which had been rearranged since he'd last been here. A circle of mismatched chairs formed a half-circle with a comfortable-looking armchair in the center. That must be for Olivia. He'd have a great view of her if he sat in the middle of the row. He claimed it by tossing Steve's plush toy on the chair. Froggie, Steve's security plushie, went everywhere Steve did. He'd had the stuffed frog since he was a puppy, and how it had survived his teething phase was a mystery.

Wyatt took a closer look at the walls, smothered in old photos. He recognized most people in them, but they weren't as interesting to him as his knitting teacher. Olivia sat on the floor across from Steve, wiping dog slobber from her glasses. She must have felt Wyatt watching her because she lifted those impossible lashes his way.

Her eyes did funny things to him.

He dropped Steve's leash. "Millie gave me permission to bring Steve, in case you were wondering."

"I'm so glad you joined us," she baby-talked Steve.

Steve swiped the side of her face with his tongue.

Olivia massaged his ears, and the dog groaned. When he closed his eyes, she giggled. "How did he get his name?" She tweaked her lips to one side when Steve flopped over on his side.

"Don't know. I guess Steve just fit him."

Steve's eyes were half-mast, and he smiled. *Smiled.* He did that sometimes, and usually it didn't annoy Waytt, but right now…

Olivia gave Steve one last kiss between his ears and stood. "I guess we'd better get started, everyone."

The other knitting students began stowing bags underneath the chairs, so Wyatt hurried to sit in the seat he'd saved.

"We have a few new faces." Olivia took charge, but her blooming cheeks told on her. She wasn't comfortable having so much attention. Or was it his attention she wasn't comfortable with?

"Welcome, everyone. Tea's in the kitchen." She indicated a refreshment table.

Once they were all seated, they took turns introducing themselves. Three elderly women sat at the end. They whispered and cut up like troublemakers in school.

Wyatt focused on Steve, who parked next to Olivia's chair and stared at her with adoration, resting his possessive paw on her knee. Wyatt looked away. Steve was either a jerk or a genius. He caught the tail end of the little old ladies' introductions. He must have misheard. How was it possible that they were all named Betty?

He was puzzling over that when Jared Huff elbowed him. Jared was the kind of guy that Wyatt would gladly sick Christine and her friends on.

"Is it my turn?" Wyatt had lost track.

One of the Betties reached across others to pat his thigh. "Yes, dear."

Wyatt cleared his throat. "I'm Wyatt Simms, I work for Wild Rose Fire and Rescue as a firefighter. Some of you know my parents, who own Quail Ridge Cellars."

"The vineyard in front of their tasting room is gorgeous right now with the fall colors coming on." Alma Higgins's comment was directed to Olivia.

Wyatt thanked her and then turned to the next person.

Introductions continued with two preteen girls and their mom, followed by a handful of thirty-somethings. They spoke about something they called granny culture. Wyatt paid attention. Who knew knitting and crocheting were prescriptions for mental health?

Just as Wyatt had hoped, Steve was popular with the ladies. His dog turned the tide on things with Olivia. Still, she was clearly unimpressed with his inability to learn simple handiwork.

Wyatt couldn't make his fingers work the knitting needles like Olivia showed them. His yarn tangled and rolled across the floor. Steve gnawed it and got it slimy. Wyatt was only half-watching his hands anyway. It was hard not to sneak peeks at Olivia as she flitted around the small circle like a butterfly, encouraging her students. Wyatt's jaw clenched when she stooped over Jared with her hair cascading down, showing him the slip knot *one more time*.

She was patient as she guided Jared's hands. "Now give the loop a little tug."

Jared, the big dope, sent a triumphant smirk across the circle

Waytt dropped one of his needles and slammed Jared with a dirty look on his way down to retrieve it. He knew precisely why Jared was here. That dude didn't want to knit a scarf.

"Steve, stop that." Wyatt tried to contain his frustration. He'd hoped being clumsy would work in his favor, but no matter how much trouble he had casting stitches, Olivia ignored his struggle.

Steve put a clumsy paw over the mess of needles and yarn that slipped from Wyatt's grasp. Just as he was about to scold the dog, a delicate pair of hands intervened. Olivia moved Steve's paw aside with a gentle motion while swiping the yarn and needles. Wyatt swam in an intoxicating blend of clean laundry, lemons, and lavender.

Olivia dropped a kiss on the mutt, setting his tail to drumming the floor. "Who's a good boy? Steve is, aren't you, Stevie?"

Jared met Wyatt's eyes over Olivia's bent head with a scowl.

Wyatt grinned wickedly. Yep, Steve was a great idea.

Some of the ladies had finished with their lesson and began to visit. They poured tea and waited in line for the bathroom.

Olivia slipped into the empty chair next to Wyatt and gave him a shy smile. "Looks like you're having a bit of trouble. Let me help." She set her nimble fingers to undoing Wyatt's knotted-up yarn coated in Steve's slobber. She didn't even appear to mind—another point in Olivia's favor.

"What's this?" She lifted off the seat and pulled out Steve's security plushie.

"Froggie," Wyatt said. He was focused on looping his stitch. Maybe if he impressed Olivia—

Steve pulled Froggie from Olivia's hand with the gentlest mouth possible and dropped his plushie between his front feet. He didn't like anyone else to touch his favorite toy.

Olivia pressed a hand to her heart. "That's the sweetest thing I've ever seen."

Wyatt was going to grill Steve a steak when they got home.

After polishing off a plate of cookies Millie Rutherford set on the table, most other students trickled out. Millie tiptoed away after refilling a teapot, but not without a wink in Wyatt's direction. She tipped her head with a nod of approval toward the scene in the center—Steve's head in Olivia's lap, staring lovingly up as Olivia repeatedly told him what a good boy he was.

Jared's face was thunder. Wyatt gave him a suck-it-loser look on his way out.

Olivia stood and hugged the trio of old ladies at the door. "Bye, Betties."

Wyatt turned to Olivia. "Is that why they're friends?"

"What do you mean?"

Wyatt gestured. "They're all named Betty."

Her eyes twinkled, and her shoulders shook.

Wyatt's chest swelled. He'd made Olivia laugh.

When her laughing turned into hiccups, she turned to Wyatt with a smile that would have knocked him down if he hadn't been sitting. "Oh, that's funny."

"I gathered, although I'm not sure what I said to get such an amazing reaction."

"Those ladies are the Birding Betties. May, Arlene, and Teresa. There are more of us, but these were the only ones I could talk into coming to knitting class."

Wyatt dipped his chin. "Us?"

Olivia waved a hand as if brushing aside an argument. "I know they're all elderly, but they're lots of fun." Olivia's eyes were bright. She pushed her glasses up on her nose.

"The Birding Betties. Now I understand. Their meetings are held at the Sunny Day Retirement Home." Wyatt took a moment to process. "You're one of them?"

"Yep. How did you know where the meetings are held?" She tilted her head.

"I've been on a couple of calls at that facility. People fall off toilets and…never mind."

Ducking her head, Olivia blushed. Man, she was so pretty.

Wyatt ticked off a mental list of what he knew about her. She worked at a knitting shop, taught knitting classes, and belonged to a senior citizen group of bird watchers. She couldn't be more different from the fire department groupies. Unless she turned out to be a serial killer or something, he might have found the girl of his dreams.

Olivia cooed over Steve and pressed her nose to his neck. Wyatt glanced up at Morris the cat, watching it all from a beam above them, glaring with pure jealousy. Wyatt related.

He wasn't above using Steve to his advantage. "So, you're a bird watcher. Steve loves to walk the hiking trails." Wyatt pointed to his labrador, who sure loved birds, but not in the same way Olivia and the bird-watching Betties did. "We see tons of birds on our hikes, don't we, boy? I've often wished we had a hiking partner who could identify them for us." Steve lifted his ears at that.

Olivia booped Steve's nose with her fingertip and attempted to get a better look at Froggie. Steve slapped a paw over the raggedy green plushie.

"Look, Steve thinks a day hike with you is a fantastic

idea." Wyatt held back a cocky smile. Brilliant idea if he did say so.

But Olivia didn't seem enthusiastic about his plan. Her eyes darted anywhere but his face.

He was a fast thinker, though. "We keep seeing a certain rare bird. I described it to my mom—she loves birds too—and she said she thinks it might be a Black-throated Sparrow. But we'd need someone more knowledgeable to be sure."

Eyes lighting, Olivia pulled her phone from her pocket and thumbed a web search. She flipped the phone. "Is it this one?"

His bones melted at the spark in Olivia's eye. "Well...I can't be sure. You'd need to see it in person, don't you think?"

With a bashful smile, she nodded.

"How about Saturday? I'm off shift at eight a.m."

"I'll bring lunch for us," She said in a near-whisper. Then, her eyes brightened. "Is Steve allowed to have treats? There's a doggy bakery downtown that I've always wanted to check out."

Steve's ears propelled forward.

"Did you hear that, buddy? Olivia wants to spoil you." He landed a toothy smile on her. "He loves treats." He smoothed Steve's ears back down. "The three of us could check it out before we hike?"

Tugging at a strand of her hair, Olivia wet her lips. "Okay."

By the time Steve and Wyatt left *Hooked On Ewe*, they both were smitten. "Come on, Steve." He whistled and jogged for his truck.

He spotted Trish leaning against the passenger door. Her

mini-skirt showed a lot of thigh. "Knitting club?" She had one brow lifted in a way that implied mockery.

Wyatt looked over his shoulder. Was Olivia watching? He let out a breath. "Excuse us, we're kind of in a hurry." He scooted Trish aside to open the door for Steve.

"Gotta go." He went around the truck to jump in, locked the doors, and fired the engine.

## 4

---

## BIRD WATCHING

*I*t was sweater-weather in town, but at the higher elevation, the air nipped. "I haven't been up this high before," Olivia said. She snuggled into her down jacket and pulled the zipper tab.

Wyatt, walking ahead on the narrow trail, glanced back. "The woods are beautiful this time of year."

Olivia pushed her glasses up and stopped to examine a small flower on the forest floor with berry-red petals and a golden center.

He turned around. "What did you find?"

"Just a flower."

He bent for a closer look. "Pretty thing, isn't it?"

Olivia smiled an agreeable smile and wondered why she'd agreed to come when she barely had the power of thought around Wyatt. The man was dreamy and so far out of her league that she was bound to embarrass herself or have her heart crushed sooner or later.

But he was so nice...

"Just let me know when you're hungry, Olivia." Wyatt

shifted the pack carrying their lunch and water bottles. "Steve has a hollow leg, so don't bother asking him."

The grin he tossed over his shoulder made her stumble. "We can eat whenever you're hungry. You're the one who worked a twenty-four-hour shift. I can't believe you don't go home and sleep after your shift."

"Some things are worth losing sleep over."

Heat flashed across her cheeks. There must be a dozen women in Wild Rose Ridge who'd kill to be in Olivia's hiking boots right now.

She'd quaked with nerves when Wyatt picked her up from Millie's, but she began to enjoy herself once they reached the *Bowow Bakery*. Steve's exuberance in the dog treat bakery made her laugh. He was greedy, but even she had to admit the dog cookies looked good enough for people to eat. She'd picked out a dozen with Steve's help and gone up front to pay, but Wyatt slipped his debit card to the cashier before Olivia got her wallet out. He reminded her of the hero in the last romance she'd read.

Still, she kept reminding herself that it was safer to have book boyfriends than real boyfriends. She'd resigned herself to the single life after several disastrous attempts at dating in her twenties.

But Wyatt didn't seem put off by her oddities. He didn't laugh at her when she told him that she belonged to a senior citizen birdwatching club; stranger still, he took the trouble of learning to knit. Things might be different this time.

She couldn't wipe the smile from her face as she followed Wyatt up the trail. Today was perfect. If only it could last. She inhaled the bracing scent of pine as her boots crushed the needles on the ground and tried to keep her eyes out for birds. That didn't prove easy when she had such fascinating scenery on the trail in front of her. She had yet to record anything new in her birding notebook.

Steve crashed through the undergrowth to her side and startled a grouse.

"Watch out," Wyatt called.

Olivia wouldn't exactly call Steve helpful for bird watching. He flushed them out and then chased them off.

Wyatt froze and pointed. "There. I think that's it."

Olivia lifted the binoculars hanging around her neck and examined the little bird. "No, I'm afraid that isn't the Black-throated Sparrow." She gave him a sympathetic shrug. "It's a Black-capped Chickadee. They have similar plumage. It's an easy mistake." She held the binoculars out for him.

Their eyes met as he leaned into Olivia's side, pressed close to peer through the binoculars still attached to the strap around her neck. His body heat, the clean scent of soap, and the hint of aftershave made her bones go soft at close range. She grabbed hold of his arm to keep herself upright.

Wyatt handed her the binoculars, an oblivious smile. "Let's follow the trail further."

Steve growled and bolted away, breaking the spell for Olivia.

Kneeling, Wyatt examined a pile of scat a couple of feet away. "Coyote." He gave an unconcerned shrug and patted Steve. "Good boy."

Olivia shuddered. Did the Betties know about the coyotes along this trail?

"Olivia, do you have your notebook handy?" Wyatt stopped to point out a bird cleaning its beak on a knobby tree limb on the opposite side of the trail.

She didn't need her binoculars. "That's a Magpie. There are two more." She pointed to another tree.

Wyatt's shoulders drooped. Not having any practice soothing a man's pride, Olivia figured she should at least try. She closed the distance between them and reached out. "They are gorgeous though, aren't they?" Touching his arm caused her mouth to go dry.

Wyatt's eyes were winter-gray, calm, clear, and...beautiful. Olivia's thoughts scattered like the flushed grouse. She caught her foot on a tree root and toppled sideways.

"Careful." Wyatt held her elbow steady. He held her up and grinned as if he guessed the problem.

Olivia's face burned right up to her hair follicles. She backed up, smacked into a tree trunk, and bit her tongue.

"You okay?" Wyatt's concerned face blocked Olivia's view of anything else, and her senses swam in his manly scent.

Wyatt was large, masculine, and strong as he closed in to check on her. Were all firefighters so fit?

"I'm—I'm fine." That was a lie; her tongue was sore.

His breath was warm on her face, his hands gentle on her arms as he patted her. Glancing down, he frowned. "This might be your problem." He squatted to tie the laces on her hiking boot that had tangled into the brush.

"Thanks," she said around her swollen tongue.

"It's time for some water and a rest." Wyatt propelled Olivia by her elbow. "Just a little further, and we'll find a big rock where we can sit."

Steve whined and nosed Olivia's hand. She smiled, but Wyatt pushed the dog away.

"Leave her be, buddy." He turned a worried expression on Olivia.

She was struck again by the beauty of his gray eyes.

"Ready to eat?"

She hesitated. "I bit my tongue."

"Let me see." He turned into a concerned professional.

She shook her head. "I'm okay." But she tasted copper, and her eyes watered. If only she could find a magic mushroom on the ground and gobble it up like Alice in Wonderland so she could shrink. Or better yet, become invisible. The last thing she wanted was Wyatt looking in her open mouth.

"If you say so."

Wyatt got a front-row view of how awkward she was.

Olivia resigned herself that this would be their last date as well as their first.

*W*yatt devoured the ham sandwiches Olivia had packed while pretending not to stare at her beautiful profile. "These are better than my mom's." He polished off the peanut butter brownies—his and hers both— and ate a crisp apple all before Olivia managed half a sandwich.

She shared her other half with Steve. "I'm not very hungry," she explained.

She named every bird they saw for him while they ate their picnic. Wyatt had never enjoyed a hike so much. Olivia was good company.

More than good.

He wanted to know everything about her. "How did you like growing up in Kingston? What was your childhood home like?"

"Wet and rainy but beautiful. My parent's home is on the

water." A look passed over her face Wyatt couldn't read. "The wildlife was the best part of living there."

Wyatt wiped crumbs from his mouth. "You seem happy in the woods." A fact that delighted him since he loved a tromp up the trails.

The afternoon sun filtered through the branches over their heads, glinting off strands of Olivia's hair. It wasn't brown as he'd first thought, but gold and mahogany. She wore a soft fringe of bangs that drew attention to her dark brown eyes. *Those eyes.*

He was devising a plan to see them up close when Olivia turned her curious gaze his way. "What about your home? What's it like growing up in the middle of vineyards? It sounds romantic."

Wyatt chuckled. It's a lot of hard work and grubbing in the dirt."

"Quail Hollow Vineyards, right?" She leaned against the boulder behind her and pulled her collar higher. It got cold this time of day.

"That's right, I'm impressed you remembered. My father inherited the vineyard from his father. Before that, it was an apple orchard."

"You grew up working in the vineyards?"

"Yep. Apart from college and then the fire academy in North Bend." He smiled at the way Olivia fiddled with Steve's ears.

Steve snored, his boneless body stretched out alongside Olivia's legs. Wyatt rolled over onto his back, crossing his arms under his head. The breeze made the Fir trees above them sway. Here and there stood a few English walnut trees that grew wild from settler's orchards a hundred years ago. A fat squirrel ran from limb to limb before he plunked down over Wyatt's head and munched a walnut. His eyes darted between Wyatt, Olivia, and Steve as if he were watching a movie screen. His tiny paws turned the nut this way and that, and when he'd finished the nut meat, he launched the shell.

It bounced off Wyatt's forehead. "Hey!"

Olivia covered a giggle with her hand.

"Find that funny, do you?"

She nodded and let her hand drop. Her laughter was sweet, like warm honey drizzling over him.

Everything about Olivia was sweet and warm. No other woman had caught his interest so thoroughly before, At least not since his infatuation with Shelby Donavon in seventh grade. Rubbing the spot where a corner of the broken nutshell landed, Wyatt sat upright. "Tell me about the best day of your life so far."

Olivia crossed her legs at the ankles and focused on the sky above her. "Hmmmm. That's a tough question." She lifted her head. "What was yours?"

"I used to think it was the day I graduated from the academy. I'd dreamed of being a firefighter since the third grade. But actually, my happiest day was the day I brought Steve home. He was a seven-week-old pup and a lot of work, but I can't imagine my life without him now." Wyatt tossed a pinecone at Steve. Steve raised his head. "His happiest day was the day I bought Froggie."

Steve bolted up and looked around.

Olivia laughed. Steve's top lip curled under, exposing his teeth on one side, and the sleepy droop of his face made him ridiculous.

"How long ago did you get Steve?" Olivia picked dried pine needles out of Steve's coat after he settled back down.

"Five years ago."

"He's perfect." Olivia's eyes crinkled softly in the corners.

She smiled with her whole face. He liked that.

She glanced up through her lashes. "I'm on the hunt for a place of my own. I'd like to have a little farm and raise sheep."

"Sheep?"

"I want them for the fleece so I can spin my own yarn."

At his raised eyebrows, she blushed and fixed her attention on Steve. "Silly?"

"Not at all. I like sheep."

"I'd want a dog to help move the sheep from pasture to pasture." A thoughtful expression crossed her face. "I'd need a cat or two to keep the mice away. Besides, I like them."

"The shop cat isn't enough?" he joked.

"Aunt Millie's tomcat isn't the cuddly type."

"Morris? He seems friendly."

"Friendly, yes. Cuddly? No."

"My sister's cat has a litter of kittens. Would you like one of those?"

"I need a place of my own first." Olivia gave a one-shoul-dered shrug.

"There aren't a lot of rentals in Wild Rose Ridge. Most homeowners make extra income renting weekends out to winery tourists and lake enthusiasts." Wyatt shuffled through a mental list of people who might rent to a single woman.

"I realized that right away. I'm praying about it, though, so I'm sure the right place will become available." The serene smile on Olivia's face spoke to Wyatt of a strong faith underneath her shy outer layer.

"Have you found a church to attend since moving here?" He hadn't been to church much lately. His friend group stayed out late most Saturday nights, and he'd found himself waking Sunday mornings long after the family had gone to town.

"I've been attending Wild Rose Community Church with Millie since my first week here."

A rightness settled on Wyatt. "My family has gone there since my grandparents married in the original chapel."

Olivia's dark brown furrowed. "I don't remember seeing you."

It was Wyatt's turn to blush. "I haven't been consistent for a while."

"Oh."

"You might have met my parents, though."

"Does your mother teach Sunday school?"

"She sings with the worship team." He missed hearing Mom's singing.

Olivia's brows jumped up. "I knew I recognized your mother's beautiful eyes the day you and I met." A deep stain washed over Olivia's face.

He chuckled and batted his lashes her way. "Hazel has them, too."

Olivia's brows bunched.

"Hazel's my sister."

"Oh." She dropped her gaze to her hands.

He took pity on her and changed the subject. "You never told me about the best day of your life."

Olivia lifted her chin. "I'm not like you," she said. "I don't have many friends or a job that gives me an adrenaline rush—I don't even like adrenaline rushes—and I've never been popular, so my best day probably won't impress you."

Wyatt brought his knees up. "Try me."

"Well, when I turned fourteen, I got a summer job helping on a sheep farm. One of our neighbors was a widow who raised sheep for their fleece. Leota had a spinning wheel and everything. I became fascinated with raising lambs, shearing them, spinning the wool…everything having to do with creating skeins of yarn from the fleece her sheep produced. I was so impressed that she was involved in every part of the process. It was magical to me. On the days we finished chores early, Leota taught me to spin. She even trusted me with her family's sweater pattern." She began twisting a stick into a pretzel shape. "The day I finished my first sweater was my happiest day." She met Wyatt's eyes. "I loved Leota. She used to pray for me and often reminded me that God had great plans for my life. She said sometimes the best plans are the simple ones."

"Leota sounds like she was special."

Olivia gulped a big breath. "She meant the world to me. I worked hard on her farm, but I always found peace there. Leota made me feel like God saw me and…that He liked me."

"That sounds like a wonderful day." Wyatt gave Olivia his best smile. "I'd like to see that sweater sometime."

She searched his face, testing him before she gave him a smile back.

He debated for a moment and then plunged in. "You don't have a boyfriend, do you? It's just that I can't believe someone as wonderful as you is single."

Olivia opened her mouth and then closed it. Shook her head. "Do you? I mean, have a girlfriend?" She lowered her eyes. "I assumed you didn't since we're here together."

"Nope."

"I find that hard to believe," she whispered.

"My friends are a bit wild. Our jobs are dangerous and stressful. We do what others aren't able to do—or are unwilling to do—and some of us think we deserve to play hard."

"Oh."

"All that to say, it's been hard for me to find the right person."

"And what about you?" She lifted her lashes. "Do you play as hard as you work?"

"I got caught up in that culture for a while. Some of the guys party to let off steam, and others are self-medicating. I've seen those lines crossed, so I'm careful." He stretched out his legs. "I keep grounded by working with my family. My grandfather warned me not to let my identity get wrapped up in my career early on, and he was right." He rubbed the shell the squirrel had used as a missile and put it in his pocket. "I feel like I've outgrown some of my friends." He rested his eyes on Olivia's face. "I'd like to think the best is yet to come."

Olivia's fingers plucked at Steve's collar. "What do you consider the best?"

A smile tugged at Wyatt's mouth. How would Olivia react to his answer? "I'd like to meet my better half and start a family. My friends may be having fun living the single life, but it doesn't give me the same tickles it does them." He stood and brushed off his pants. The sun was sinking in a sky turning purple. "We need to head back down. What do you think about stopping at the Rose & Thorn for dinner?"

He liked being with Olivia, and if they ended the date right after their hike, he wouldn't see her until he returned to inspect Hooked On Ewe. Tomorrow, he'd promised Dad he'd help him with some troublesome vines, and the day after, he had a twenty-four-hour shift at the fire department.

That was too long without Olivia's company.

Hesitating, she stretched out a reluctant answer with an uncertain smile. "Okay, I've never been to the Rose & Thorn."

"Great. I can't wait for you to meet some of the guys." He held out a hand to help her up and caught sight of a retreat in her eyes he'd seen the day he met her.

Maybe taking her to the alehouse wasn't the best idea, but if they were to get serious, she'd have to fit into his life as much as he'd have to fit into hers.

## 5

### IF AT FIRST YOU DON'T SUCCEED…

The Rose & Thorn Alehouse was packed.

Olivia's mouth went dry as Wyatt held the door open for her. She tried to calm her breathing as Wyatt pressed his hand on the small of her back to steer her to the last empty table in the corner of the chaos. His touch made her knees rubbery. It was either that or the people who unnerved her. So many people.

"It's a busy night." Wyatt gave her an apologetic look and held a chair out for her.

"Wyatt, over here." A disheveled man waved in their direction. He swayed at the head of two tables pushed together, cluttered with pitchers and glasses where a dozen men and a few women sat.

Wyatt waved back and shook his head. The man made a rude gesture and collapsed with laughter, landing on his backside when he missed the chair behind him.

Wyatt sighed. "Sorry. They've been here a while."

"How can you tell?" Olivia snuck a peek at the rowdy group. The women eyed her.

"Joey's had a few beers too many."

"Is he the one that…"

"Yes. Joey's been my best friend since middle school. We went through the academy together." He glanced toward his friend, fumbling to get upright. "He's changed a lot since then."

Was Joey perhaps one of the friends Wyatt mentioned outgrowing? Turning, she held her breath while Joey stood on a chair and chugged the remainder of a mostly full pitcher. "Oh. Your best friend." Maybe this part of their date had been a mistake.

"I know he doesn't seem like much now, but Joey's a great guy." Wyatt retreated from Olivia's gaze. "The menu's right here." He held out a sheet of cardstock from behind a rack with Tobasco sauce, salt, pepper, and sugar packets. When their hands brushed, the touch gave Olivia a little jolt.

"The burgers are amazing, but so's the pizza. They have a real woodfire oven in the back."

Olivia tugged a napkin from the dispenser and wiped at the smears on the menu. Her hands trembled a little, but she reminded herself that she'd wanted to get out more and meet people her age. This was Wyatt's hangout, those people were his friends, and she liked him. She could do this.

"Hot wings and potato wedges sound wonderful."

A slow grin took over Wyatt's handsome face. "I wouldn't have taken you for a spicy girl."

"I'm full of surprises." She certainly surprised herself.

She was on a date.

With the swooniest man she'd ever met.

At a pub.

Mom would decide there was hope for her yet, but she would disapprove of the obnoxious drunks Wyatt called friends.

Elbows on the table, Wyatt leaned closer. "Your eyes have little flecks of gold, like your hair."

She was tempted to close her eyes to escape Wyatt's intensity. His warm breath made her belly quiver. "Your eyes have shots of silver in the gray."

Had she just said that out loud?

Wyatt slid his hands to the middle of the table with a question in the curve in his brow, and after a breath, she slid her hands to meet his. His warm fingers laced with hers and pulled her closer. Her heart rapid-fired in her chest, but lucky for her, the Rose & Thorn was so loud he couldn't possibly hear it.

She'd only been kissed once. And it hadn't even been a good kiss, either. Kissing Kevin Smith was not unlike kissing a dead fish. She hadn't bothered to let him try again, and since he broke up with her shortly after, it probably hadn't been her best effort either.

A blonde woman in a tiny dress and big earrings dug her fingernails into Wyatt's arm as she tottered at their table. "Well, well. Wyatt, what—I mean who—do we have here?" Her eye makeup slid down her cheeks, and her lips curled into a sneer when she landed her glassy coal eyes on Olivia.

Olivia cringed at the woman's glare but caught herself and straightened. She had to stop being such a coward. She pulled her hand away from Wyatt and held it out. "I'm Olivia Lewis." She gave the woman a tight smile. "And you're…?"

"Chris." It came out as a hiss.

*Appropriate.*

"Chris?" Olivia lifted the edge of her brow.

Chris turned her back. "Who's your new little friend, Wyatt?"

Wyatt's nostrils flared. "I believe Olivia just introduced

herself." He stood and placed gentle hands on Chris's shoulders. He turned her toward the table where all their friends sat. "I think you're lost, Christine." He waved a hand toward the group. "Hector, it's time to give Chris a ride home."

The man Wyatt called Hector snatched a purse from the back of the chair next to him and held it out. "Come on, Christine. Let's get you girls home."

Olivia had never been around drunk people, and she didn't like it much. Wyatt seemed annoyed by his friends, but surely he might have expected this scene. She pointed to Hector. "Is that her boyfriend or her brother?"

"Neither. Hector's a medic on my shift. He looks out for the drunks because he never drinks."

"He's the designated driver?"

"Something like that."

"She doesn't look like she's capable of good decisions right now." Olivia crossed her arms.

"Hector isn't the kind of guy to take advantage of a woman in her condition." He slid the menus back behind the salt shaker. "Would you like to find someplace quieter?"

"I'm not hungry anymore. Could you take me back to my aunt's house?"

Her heart fell at Wyatt's disappointed expression. She liked him, but his world would be impossible for her. She stood and zipped her jacket up. She made her way to the entrance, expecting Wyatt to stop to talk to his friends, but he stayed close, even clearing a path for her.

"I'm sorry, Olivia." His shoulders were hunched as they walked to his truck at the curb.

Steve's head popped out the window, and he wagged his tail, reminding Olivia there was more to Wyatt Simms than his drinking buddies. She reached through the open window and stroked Steve's head. "You're a good boy, aren't you?

Yes, you are." She rifled in her jacket pocket for a dog treat and produced a glazed squirrel cookie. "Here you go, boy."

Steve smacked his lips and gobbled the squirrel.

Olivia caught Wyatt watching her. "I'm the one who's sorry. Your friends are just having fun. I'm…I'm boring." She held her hands up in a helpless gesture.

He took a step closer. "You're not boring. You like things different from those guys, and that's okay. Birds are cool, and hey, I liked knitting class."

"No, you didn't."

The teasing smile he gave her stopped her heart, but the smile fell away, and his expression turned serious. "I'd like to see you again," he said.

"You would?" Sitting with Wyatt inside the Rose & Thorn was like high school all over.

"I'd *love* to see you again."

Olivia pushed her glasses up with her finger. She rubbed Steve's ears. The silence stretched to an uncomfortable length of time.

Finally, Wyatt covered a cough with his hand. "We can talk when I come to inspect the shop again." He opened the truck door. "Stay, Steve."

Olivia climbed into the truck beside Steve and wrapped her arm around his neck. Why did she always have to chicken out of a good thing? The ride home was awkward, but Steve sat between them like a buffer from the disappointment that radiated from Wyatt's side of the truck.

Olivia was also plenty disappointed—in herself. Wyatt might really like her and think he wants to see her again, but sooner or later, he'd realize they were too different, and even if he could forget that, his friends wouldn't let him.

*W*yatt opened the door to Hooked On Ewe with squared shoulders and determination. He was here to inspect the shop again, but his motives weren't all business. After some hard thinking and a talk with Dad, he'd decided to persuade Olivia that they owed it to themselves to try again.

He'd actually ironed his uniform shirt last night in preparation for today. His uniform gave him confidence and changed how people treated him, and he couldn't deny it came in handy when he wanted to impress someone.

Good-time-Joey came in behind him waving his hand in front of his face. "Whew. What's that stink?"

Giving him an elbow, Wyatt threw him a warning glance that said I'll-throat punch-you-if-you-don't-shut-up. "That's lavender, you dolt."

Joey held a hand to his ear. "What's that racket?"

"Classical music." Wyatt rolled his eyes.

"It's stupid."

Wyatt turned to face his friend. "You might try to be professional once in a while, Joey. You're a public servant in uniform." Joey was still ticked about Wyatt not hanging out with him Saturday night. He might not be ready to grow up, but Wyatt was.

Joey picked invisible lint from his uniform and straightened his badge. "Alright, professional you want, professional you shall get." He took long-legged strides to the cash register where Millie Rutherford helped a pair of little old ladies bag up their yarn haul. "Excuse me, official business. My partner and I are here to go over a failed safety inspection from last week."

The ladies pressed hands to their bosoms and stepped aside. Wyatt sighed. At least he hadn't been assigned to work with Lieutenant Moore today.

Millie Rutherford frowned at Joey. "I'll be with you shortly."

Wyatt grinned when the orange tabby—stretched out on the counter like a model—snagged the edge of Joey's uniform shirt with his claws. Joey's allergies were kicking in already, and he struggled to free himself. The more he pulled, the more the cat yanked at the fabric.

Wyatt chuckled and headed for the back wall. Stacks of boxes three and four high were scattered near empty cubbies. Today must be a restocking day. Maybe that was the reason Olivia hadn't answered any of his texts. He passed the boxes of yarn and found Olivia kneeling to open a box.

She grabbed attention in a green sweater and jeans that ended above the ankle with her messy and wild hair piled on her head. She turned, pushing up her glasses as she focused on him. "Oh. It's you."

*Ouch.* Wyatt presented her with his most charming smile. He indicated the full yarn cubbies. "Been busy, I see."

Olivia stood and clasped her hands together. She shot a glance toward the front of the shop. "Is that your friend from the pub?"

"Yep. Only Joey's on duty, so you'll like him better today." *Maybe.* He reached for a packet on the floor. "You dropped these." He turned the package over. "They don't look like knitting needles."

"Those are crochet hooks."

"Do you know how to use them? They look dangerous."

When she took it from him, he glimpsed amusement in her eyes. "I make socks with these."

He puffed out his chest a little because clearly, she was

warming to him." Maybe I'd do better with a crotchet hook than knitting needles. Will you show me how to crochet on Thursday?" He pictured Jared Huff's jealous glares and it warmed his insides. Jared wouldn't hog Olivia's undivided attention this week in knitting class.

"Alma Higgins is more skilled than I am. She could—"

"I'd learn better from you." He interrupted before she could pawn him off on Ms. Higgins.

"Well…" she hedged.

"I like your sweater; it makes your eyes pop. I mean, they're already pretty, but... what's that shade of green called?"

Olivia flushed pink. "Thanks. I just finished it." She pulled at the sweater. "It's olive green." Turning, she pulled a skein of yarn from a cubby nearby. "This color."

Wyatt took the yarn from her hand and held it up. "What do you think? Would this color suit me?"

"Y-yes." Olivia pushed up her glasses. She did that when she was nervous.

"If I buy some crochet needles and a bunch of this yarn, will you help me make a sweater?" Wyatt was willing to try anything.

"Are you serious?"

"You doubt my sincerity?" He widened his eyes.

"A little," she said with a hint of tease.

Joey strode over, jabbing at the ceiling. "Your boss says you're going to help us with the inspection. Have the smoke detectors been replaced?"

Wyatt stepped between Joey and Olivia. "This is Olivia Lewis. Olivia, this is firefighter Joe Tanner."

With a cocky smile, Joey held out a hand. "I believe we've met."

"Yes, we have." Olivia took a step back. "The smoke

detectors only needed new batteries." She set the crotchet hooks down. "Come with me, and I'll show you the other things on the list."

Ten minutes later, Olivia seemed ready to cry, and Joey was exasperated. Wyatt wanted to choke him out for upsetting Olivia.

"I can't understand it. I screwed those cover plates on myself. I made sure none of the switches were exposed. I read the citations carefully," she said with a shaky voice.

Wyatt put a comforting hand on her shoulder. "I'm sure those just slipped your notice." He jerked a thumb to the backroom, riddled with fire code violations.

Olivia stiffened. "No. I was thorough."

Millie Rutherford sauntered over with the orange cat draped over her fleshy arm. "I'm afraid that's my fault."

"Aunt Millie? What's going on? I know I fixed all those things on Friday. I'm sure I didn't overlook anything."

Millie shrugged. "Perhaps the knitting club got a little crazy. Who knows what those women get up to after a few pots of tea."

Understanding dawned, and Wyatt could kiss Millie for meddling rather than be annoyed. On the other hand, Olivia seemed oblivious to her aunt's mischief.

Millie waved her hand dismissively. "Don't worry. I'll hire a handyman to come and get us up to code." She shot Wyatt a coy look. "Unless Wyatt has time to help you when he gets off shift tomorrow?"

She was doing him a favor, and they both knew it.

Joey's eyes darted between Millie and Wyatt, and he scowled. "I'm afraid off-duty assistance isn't the department's responsibility—"

Wyatt dodged Joey's surly refusal on his behalf. "I'd be glad to help."

Millie Rutherford's monkeyshines could only help his cause. He'd send flowers to thank her.

Joey shoved his clipboard in Wyatt's gut and stalked out of the shop, shaking his head and muttering.

Eyes following Joey's back, Olivia slumped. "He thinks I'm lying."

"No. He doesn't. Listen, let's make a deal. I'll make sure Hooked On Ewe passes the next inspection, and you teach me to crochet a sweater." Making a sweater probably took several weeks and even longer if he proved to be a slow learner.

Millie beamed. "That's a lovely idea. Wonderful. Yes. Come on your next day off, dear. I'll bake muffins. Blueberry or chocolate chip?" She let the cat slide out of her arms and melt onto the carpet in a furry puddle. "Or do you like cupcakes? Olivia is the real baker in our family."

Olivia's eyes widened. "I don't know how to—"

"It's settled then. We'll bake muffins." Millie scuttled back to the cash register, where the line was three people deep. She looked at them over her shoulder with a sly smile. "Olive green would suit you, Wyatt."

Olivia made a little choking sound and blushed. "I'm so sorry," she whispered.

Chuckling, Wyatt reached down to pet the cat. When he stood upright, he caught Olivia's eyes. "I like your aunt. And I like you."

Her gaze dropped to her feet. "I...you..."

"Pardon?" He didn't quite catch her mumbled response.

Lifting her gorgeous brown eyes and pushing up her glasses, Olivia's chin jutted out. "I said, I like you, too."

A huge grin split his face. "Good. Great. I mean, I'm glad." He slipped his hands in his pockets and rocked back on the heels of his uniform boots. "Then how about lunch at Frog Legs Grill tomorrow?"

"I have to work."

"Dinner then?"

"Do we have to eat frog legs?"

Wyatt laughed. "Nope."

"I'm not sure." She raised her eyebrows toward the window where Joey leaned against the fire truck.

"I'd like to try." He willed her to say yes. "It's only dinner."

"I get off at six."

He wanted to punch the air in victory. "Before I go, I'd like to buy yarn and a crochet hook." He loaded the crook of an arm with olive green yarn.

"You'll need a bigger hook." Olivia pointed to a wall lined with knitting needles, crochet hooks, and other things he couldn't identify. She lifted a package from the wall and offered it to Wyatt. His pulse spiked when their fingers touched.

They smiled into each other's eyes, and Olivia's breath hitched audibly.

"Hey! You coming or what?"

But Joey spoiled their moment. He was getting good at that.

# 6

## PUMPKIN SPICE IS NICE

*O*livia paused at the backdoor of Hooked On Ewe to reposition the plate of warm-from-the-oven pumpkin spice muffins. Voices coming from inside meant Millie was still there, so Olivia didn't have to set everything down to search for her keys. Her ears perked up when she reached for the knob and heard her name.

"No need for you to come here, I'm keeping Liv busy, and she's making friends. Very social these days, yes. Well, there's the Harvest Festival and a rodeo." Millie could only be talking to Mom.

Olivia rolled her shoulders and blew out a breath. Of course, Mom wanted to come here and push Olivia harder to conform to her idea of the perfect daughter. It was a nuisance to be shy and awkward. That much Olivia would agree with. She didn't exactly aspire to be the most boring person at every party.

"She's met someone. Well, he's a firefighter and so handsome. The thing is, Olivia doesn't have what it takes. No, I mean she doesn't make much effort. The others and I have helped a bit…"

Olivia pressed her lips together. What was Millie up to? Olivia heard rumors about the Meddling Mamas, but that was just a joke around town.

"I've got someone on it. No, don't drive over. I haven't got room for you to stay." Mom pushed Millie, too.

A loud knock on the front door interrupted the phone conversation.

"I've got to go. Someone's at the door. No, the shop door. Bye now." Millie's footsteps rushing to the front of the shop meant Olivia could come through the back door without catching her in the act of colluding with the enemy.

She didn't like confrontations.

Wyatt's deep voice from the front of the store kicked Olivia's heart into racing speed. He had that effect on her. She could hardly believe he'd returned, expecting him to disappear like any sensible man after the tense day they'd spent getting the shop fit to pass inspection. The poor guy hadn't slept a wink, and Millie followed them around the entire time, making not-so-subtle innuendos about love and marriage. By the end of the day, Olivia's nerves were shot. She canceled their dinner plans, saying she had a headache. It wasn't a lie.

She set down the muffins and checked her watch. Wyatt was early for class.

Racing to the small bathroom, she flipped on the light and checked the mirror. Her eyes were still red from the drops the eye doctor put in them at her appointment during her lunch break. She took off her glasses and squinted, trying to see herself without them. She'd had them so long she wouldn't even recognize herself without them, but it was time to try contact lenses.

Footsteps coming near made her jump away from the mirror. She slipped her glasses over her ears, smoothed her hair, and flipped the light switch. Hurrying to the tea kettle, she resumed getting ready for her students instead of examining her face at close range in the bathroom mirror.

She carried the kettle to the tiny, open kitchen Uncle Walt built before he passed and held the kettle under the tap. When the kettle was full, she set it on its base and turned it on to boil.

Wyatt's cologne wafted from behind her and pulled in as much as her lungs would hold. She let it out to the count of ten, ready to smile at Wyatt.

"Smells good in here," Wyatt said. He closed his eyes—missing Olivia's forced smile—and sniffed.

Steve plunked down with his snout in the air.

"I made muffins. The butter's on the table." Olivia made the pumpkin spice just in case Wyatt showed up. She suspected pretending her treacherous heart hadn't attached itself to Wyatt Simms like grapevines wrapped around a trellis was futile.

Somehow, he'd begun to matter to her happiness. She snuck a peek at him and sighed. He was even handsome while buttering muffins.

Once she turned thirty, she'd resigned herself to being alone. It wasn't all bad. With hardly anywhere to go most evenings, she didn't worry about shaving her legs or applying make-up.

But she wasn't the same person since moving to Wild Rose Ridge. She didn't want to give in to her fears and stay lonely. She wasn't sure who she wanted to be, but the old Olivia was gone, and good riddance.

"Olivia, that was your mother on the phone a minute ago. She sends her love." Millie pushed the butter dish closer. "Wyatt, I'm so glad to see a young man stick to knitting. You know, long ago, all sailors knitted. It kept them sane when they were away for months at sea." She set out a bowl of sugar. "I suppose it was also handy to know how to knit yourself a scarf onboard a ship in freezing winter waters."

"That would certainly be a useful skill." Wyatt grinned. "Olivia's teaching me to crotchet."

"Wonderful," Millie's voice held a note of triumph.

Olivia poured boiling water into the Brown Betty teapot, added four teabags, and tugged a knitted cozy over it. She set the pot in the middle of the tea table to brew a comforting herbal blend.

She might as well ask and get it over. "How's Mom doing?" Millie didn't know Olivia overheard the sister's phone conversation.

"Just fine. She wanted my recipe for plum jam, is all."

It was easier to go along with her. "Did she mention anything about a visit?"

"No." Millie fiddled with her earring. "Why?"

"No reason. Just curious."

Millie was definitely meddling.

"These muffins are still warm." The pleasure in Wyatt's voice made Olivia's heart glow.

"I baked them before coming to class." She shrugged a shoulder like baking was no big deal, but the truth was that she'd destroyed the kitchen, burned her arm, and fed the first batch to the garbage can.

"May I have another?"

His question made all the trouble worth it. "Have as many as you like."

Wyatt pulled a muffin apart, popped half into his mouth, and examined the other half. "Did you use real pumpkin instead of canned?"

"I grew a few pumpkins in Millie's back garden and thought...well, I know you like pumpkin."

Wyatt's brows inched up. "You grew the pumpkins and then made homemade muffins with them?" He held his third muffin to the light. "Wow. You're quite the little farmer, Liv."

Olivia hated that her cheeks still got hot when embarrassed or uncomfortable. Still, she met Wyatt's admiring gaze with her chin up. "Thank you."

Millie wore an innocent expression. "Isn't she a genius? Olivia always wanted to grow up to be a farmer."

A bald-faced lie.

Olivia stifled a groan. Why did she have to exaggerate? Keeping a garden was nothing like growing wine grapes, and cultivating a pumpkin patch didn't make Olivia a farmer.

Wyatt smacked his lips. "These are tastier than the ones they sell at Weaver's Bakery, and that's saying a lot."

Millie turned her head when the bells on the front door jingled. She squinted at the clock. "I hear knitting students coming in, so I'll go now. Have a nice time, kids." She swung her purse over her shoulder and snatched a muffin on her way out the back door. "Oh, by the by. Do you have a shift at the fire station tomorrow, Wyatt?"

"No, why?"

She slanted a smile. "No reason." She started walking away but paused mid-stride like she'd just then thought of something. "Olivia, I need you to pick up some bags of fleece in the morning at Swensen's Sheep Farm."

Wyatt's eyes lit up. "Mr. Swensen's our neighbor. I can do that for you."

Millie shook her head. "Oh no, I couldn't trouble you. Besides, I think Olivia would enjoy the sheep. She's always wanted to keep a flock of her own."

Wyatt turned to look at Olivia. "Would you like me to drive you to the farm and introduce you to Mr. Swensen?"

Olivia nodded, although she had made plans to go birding with the Betties the previous day.

"Cool," Wyatt said. He held an arm out to Millie. "Let me walk you out."

He snapped his fingers at Steve, lounging on the shop sofa. "Come on, buddy. You know you don't belong on Millie's furniture."

With exaggerated reluctance, Steve slithered off the sofa and turned sad eyes on the treats as he passed.

Olivia stepped forward and put her hand on Steve's back. "Can Steve stay with me? I haven't seen him all week."

Shrugging, Wyatt opened the door. "What do you say, boy? Want to hang out with Liv?"

Olivia kneeled on the floor, hiding a morsel of muffin behind her back. Steve plopped in front of her for an ear scratch. As soon as Wyatt and Millie walked out the door, she slipped Steve the bite of muffin.

He chomped it and licked his lips, looking for more.

"Greedy thing, you nearly took my finger," Olivia scolded. But then she bent down to kiss the top of his soft head. Dare she admit that a secret part of her was thrilled Wyatt's dog liked her? That Wyatt refused to give up on a dating relationship as easily as she did?

Wyatt's face appeared at the back door. "Liv, I'm sorry, but I got called in for overtime. There's a fire." His sincere apology was written all over his face.

"I guess that happens in your line of work." She stood up and held her shoulders back even though they wanted to slump.

"Come on, Steve." Wyatt gave a soft whistle.

"Does he have to go?"

"I'd better drop him off with my brother. He's in town, and I don't know how long my shift will be."

Olivia gave the reluctant dog a little push and forced herself to smile. "Stay safe."

Steve trotted out.

"You get used to it."

Olivia jumped and turned to see Lydia Vick, a middle-aged woman who'd come to class several times.

"Firefighters marry their jobs, and their co-workers become their family." Lydia's tone spoke of loneliness and heartache.

Olivia should say something, but what? She wasn't even Wyatt's girlfriend, let alone more. She pushed her glasses up. "Are you related to a firefighter?"

"My husband is the fire chief."

Lydia gave Olivia something to think about…another reason to guard her heart.

*W*yatt tugged off his fire-retardent gloves and wiped the sweat from his face, wincing at the salty sting in his eyes.

The rest of the exhausted fire crew sprawled around the bay floor. Some snored—asleep where they'd dropped. It had been a long night fighting a wildfire. Those who were awake were filthy and starving.

Joey sat hard on the engine step and held his head in his hands.

Peering into the side mirror, Wyatt did his best to wipe soot from his eyes. The bay door roared open to admit volunteers arriving with food for the crew. They were a welcome sight. The spicy, meaty aroma of Mexican food roused the limp crew.

He recognized Enrique, the owner of Jumping Beans restaurant, walking beside a cart loaded with foil containers. Enrique was all smiles. "Congratulations, friends. A job well done. Thank you for keeping our homes and businesses safe." He gestured to the cart with a flourish. "Now, come and eat. I brought tamales and enchiladas!"

Wyatt was too tired to eat even though his stomach growled like a predator at the tantalizing, spicy scents that overpowered the stench of smoke in the bay. He stood aside as the rest of the crew dragged themselves up to take the plates Enrique's servers held out, eating with soot-stained hands.

Joey stood with a moan and swayed. "Grab us a plate, Wyatt? My head hurts."

Clenching his hands, Wyatt faced him. "It's no wonder, drinking the night before a shift. You're hungover, and you were slow out there last night."

"Lay off, Judge and Jury. I needed some fun."

"Yeah? How fun do you think it would be to have to knock on Bellman's door and tell his wife and kids that he died fighting fire? Or how about facing Madeline's husband to notify him that she'd been badly burned—because she almost was—due to negligence on your part?"

Joey swung around, fists balled, glaring at Wyatt.

Wyatt held his ground. When had Joey become so irresponsible? "Look, we've been friends forever, but someone needs to tell you that your partying has gotten out of hand. Fighting fires is dangerous. Why risk more by—"

"Shut up, Wyatt. Just shut your mouth." Joey's hands trembled.

Wyatt took his best friend's measure and then called out. "I need a medic over here."

Matt Brewster set his plate aside. "What's up?"

"Joey needs I.V. fluids."

Matt's long legs made short work of crossing the bay. He reached for Joey's wrist to check his pulse, but Joey jerked his hand away. Lieutenant Moore stalked over, eyes dropping to Joey's hands. His brows cinched together. "Give it over."

Joey cut a glance at Wyatt, pupils flared with rage, but he held his wrist out.

Matt found Joey's pulse. "High and thready." He grasped Joey's hand. "Clammy." He jerked his chin up. "Dehydration and exhaustion. I can set him up with a bag of fluids in the back of my rig."

Moore shook his head. His eyes narrowed on Joey. "Give him a bottle of water and a bite to eat, then send him to the E.R." The ice in his tone put to death any challenge Joey might have given. "I expect firefighters on the line to take better care of themselves. Lives depend on it." He pinned Joey with a knowing look. "Your job depends on it."

Hector came over with enchiladas and rice. Joey took the plate and sat with it in his lap, glaring at the whitewashed brick wall.

Wyatt moved to sit beside him, but Joey spat on the floor. "Thanks, man."

"You think I want to have to be the one to knock on your mom's door to tell her you're dead?" He eyed the sooty glob of spit on the ground at his feet. When did his best friend become such a jerk?

Since Joey wasn't in the mood to listen, Wyatt walked away.

After stripping off his bunker gear, he hung it on a peg to be washed, snagged clean clothes from his locker inside the firehouse, and hit the shower. He'd talk to Joey about his drinking another time. Booze landed him in the emergency room this time, but next time, it might cost him his skin, his life, or the life of someone else.

After washing off the grime of last night's fire in the shower, Wyatt returned to the bay. Maybe he'd be lucky, and there'd be some food left. His stomach complained at the scent of beef drenched in red chile sauce and fresh tortillas.

Matt's ambulance was usually parked behind the first door of the bay, but since the spot was vacant, Wyatt assumed the medic had taken Joey to the hospital. Enrique had left, but one of the servers was still there, and he plated up the last gooey enchilada alongside a heaping scoop of refried beans. At Wyatt's appreciative nod of approval, he poured the last bit of red sauce over everything.

"You eat up," he said.

"Thanks—" Wyatt squinted at his nametag "— Ernesto."

He sopped up the spicy sauce with a bit of the last remaining tortilla underneath the tinfoil cover.

Fighting fire was not as glamorous as movies made it look. Wyatt fumbled in his pockets for the keys to his truck and frowned. He wasn't clear-headed and probably too tired to drive home. He left the bay with the thought of forty winks in the cab of his truck. He stumbled to a wooden bench under the flagpole to eat.

"Wyatt?"

He lifted his head; weariness slowed his thinking, but his pulse doubled at the sight of Olivia, and a smile tugged at his tired mouth. "You're a sight."

He patted the bench.

"For sore eyes?" Olivia sat beside him.

"Your poor eyes are all red, Wyatt." Olivia lifted his chin and examined his face. She'd forgotten to be shy around him. "I brought my car. Let me drive you home."

"Can I finish eating first?"

"Of course. Can I keep you company while you do?"

"Are you hungry?" Ernesto still had a container of rice and beans.

"I just ate, but thanks."

Olivia's presence next to him was comforting. Much of his tension and fatigue melted away as she talked to him. He didn't know what she was saying but was happy to hear her voice. As he wolfed the delicious enchilada down, exhaustion took over, and it was a struggle not to let his head dip.

Olivia took his plate to the garbage can and helped him load his duffel into her little car. On the drive, more to stay awake than anything else, he told Olivia about Joey.

Her reaction wasn't the one he'd expected. She whispered a prayer. "Lord, You know that Joey needs Jesus in his life. He's hurting for some reason. I pray that You would give him peace."

Wyatt's throat tightened. "Thank you." Why hadn't he thought to pray for his friend?

The tender smile she sent him dissolved his guilt. He'd think about Joey's escalating behavior later, and when he did, he'd remember to pray for him.

When they reached Quail Hollow, Olivia set the car in Park and twisted around, reaching for a bag in the back-seat. "I made something for you and Steve." She faced him with flushed cheeks.

Wyatt cocked his brows because the rest of him was too tired to move.

Olivia lifted a sweater out of the bag. Wyatt rubbed his gritty eyes. It matched the one she was wearing. "Try it on."

"Oh." He blinked.

"I know you're working on one, but I just thought…"

He did his best to look appreciative. "I like it. Twinning is winning, right?"

Olivia's sparkling eyes made his heart lurch.

"And," she said, "I made one for Steve so we can all match at the harvest festival." She held a smaller sweater up.

He tugged the tight sweater over his head.

The guys were going to destroy him over this.

Suddenly, his brother's face appeared in the window. "You must be Olivia?" Pete grinned with malice. "Mom's been dying to have you over." He stood and turned his back to them. "Mom! Wyatt's home, and he's got Olivia with him."

Olivia's face fell.

Pete leaned in. "Come on, you two. Show us those matching sweaters."

Turning to Oliva, Wyatt sighed. "I'm sorry."

She held the door handle with white knuckles, but with a quick squeeze of Wyatt's hand, Olivia climbed out of the V.W. Bug and slammed the door.

Wyatt loosened the sweater around his neck, opened the door, and unfolded his legs to stand and face his brother's mockery.

Steve came bounding out of the vines and rushed Olivia with a waggling bum.

"Hey, boy," Olivia crooned. "I have something for you, too." She held the sweater she'd made for him and let him smell it.

Pete's eyes bugged, and he slammed his hand over his mouth. Wyatt shot him a warning glare and shook his head. If Pete embarrassed Olivia, Wyatt would knock his perfect front teeth down his throat.

Pete's chin trembled with laughter, but he fixed his face as he watched Olivia struggle with the big labrador. The mutt didn't seem any happier about the situation than Wyatt, but Pete was in stitches—and not the kind used to knit sweaters.

"There." Olivia straightened and wiped the sweat from her forehead. "What do you think?" It had taken some effort to get Steve's legs into the holes.

Steve plunked down, his eyes telling a story about his feelings regarding the woman he considered his friend trussing him up.

"He loves it. I can tell." Pete shoved his hands in his pockets and gave Olivia a straight-faced lie.

## 7

ROASTED

*O*livia stumbled when Wyatt's mother embraced her. "You must be here for Wyatt's birthday celebration." She gave an extra squeeze, flattening Olivia's lungs.

Righting herself, Olivia gently pulled away and turned to meet Wyatt's eyes. He gave her a weary smile and half a shrug. "I forgot."

"You forgot today is your birthday?"

He nodded, but before he could say more, his mother rushed him with a concerned expression. "Oh, honey. You were on that fire last night, weren't you?" She turned around and shouted. "Peter, your son is home, and it looks like he's been up all night."

Mr. Simms appeared from behind a grapevine, startling Oliva. While he questioned Wyatt, she took the opportunity to peek around. The vineyards were tidy, starting right up to the front, with only the dirt driveway separating them. Turning her head for a better view, she sucked in a breath. The vines went on and on. There were hundreds. On closer inspection, they were divided and marked by varieties of wine grapes: reds, pinks, purples, and another section of pale yellow.

The vineyard sloped downhill with signs leading visitors to the tasting room. Behind her, an expansive lawn stretched like a park, bordered by fragrant lavender and soft, pink roses. The flowers made a magical path in front of the charming farmhouse. A fading vegetable garden to one side looked about ready to be put to bed for the winter except for a riotous melon patch.

Wyatt's father wiped a grubby hand across his forehead and then offered the hand to Olivia.

She gave him a limp smile and shook it. "Nice to meet you, Mr. Simms."

"We've heard a lot about you. We're glad to *finally* meet you." He shot a glance at Wyatt.

Mrs. Simms fussed over Wyatt the way mothers of sons did. "You're swaying on your feet, son. Come on inside, and I'll get you something to drink." Over her shoulder, she motioned to Olivia to follow them. "Can I offer you a lavender iced tea?"

The interior of the home wasn't what Olivia expected. She'd imagined it would be lived in, perhaps a bit messy, with everyone in the family living and working in the same space. But the walls were white and bare, the windows sparkled with sunshine and scrubbing, and the furnishings looked expensive in creams and beige shades. The hardwood floor was probably old like the house, but it was scrupulously clean, with only a sheepskin in front of the fireplace. Family photos lined up across the mantel told the family's history.

Olivia shot Wyatt a questioning look, but before he could point out who was who in the photos, his mother was at Olivia's elbow with a glass of tea.

Olivia spent the next two hours with the Simms family. The shyness that often plagued her disappeared in their home. They poked fun, told jokes and stories, and consumed indecent amounts of cake—which she couldn't complain about. It was a truly enjoyable time.

"Call me Gloria, sweetheart." Mrs. Simms, affectionate with her family, extended the same warmth to Olivia. She'd never felt this welcome in her own home growing up, and it was a comforting feeling.

"Leave her alone, Pete." Their sister, Hazel, took an immediate interest in Olivia and stuck up for her whenever Pete gave her a hard time.

"It's your turn, slowpoke." Pete teased, but it didn't put her off. Wyatt's siblings were amazing--genuinely fun.

"It's okay, Hazel. Pete's just a sore loser." She passed the Yahtzee dice. The tension in her body relaxed, leaving her free to enjoy the Simms household and wish the tiniest bit that she'd grown up in this family. "I don't remember ever having so much fun," Olivia admitted.

Pete jerked a thumb toward the other sofa, where Wyatt was sound asleep with his mouth open. "Speaking of loser."

Hazel tossed a potato chip at Pete's head. "These two. The wisecracks never end. They squabble over everything."

Olivia lifted a brow. "What do you mean?"

"It's always police versus firefighters with those two." Hazel rolled the dice and counted out her score.

"Firefighting and police work are both very respectable careers," Mrs. Simms asserted.

"You're a policeman, Pete?" Olivia didn't bother to hide her surprise.

Wyatt was taller, but Pete was broader in the chest and shoulders. They both looked like younger versions of Mr. Simms.

"Pete's a cop because he couldn't pass the fire exam." Wyatt sat up and yawned.

"Yeah, right." Pete scoffed.

"You two stop before you scare Olivia off," Mrs. Simms admonished. "Pass the chips, please, dear." She smiled, and Olivia was grateful for all the ways Wyatt's mom found to include her.

She'd just had the second-best day of her life.

Later, back at Millie's, she reflected on the day with her heart spilling over.

"So, it's Wyatt's birthday, and you didn't know?" Millie passed the popcorn bowl underneath Morris's twitching whiskers. "Uh-uh. No, you don't, mister." She brushed away his pilfering paw.

Olivia snuggled deeper and gave Morris a scratch. "Yep. I'm glad I made those matching sweaters for him and Steve. I wouldn't have had a gift ready for his birthday otherwise."

They were cozy in Millie's living room, enjoying an *I Love Lucy* marathon. The September night was chilly, but rather than light a fire, they sat on the sofa in a cuddle puddle with hand-knitted afghans. Mom would die before she'd have anything so tacky in her house. Everything was magazine-worthy and picture-perfect.

Millie settled the bowl between them. "And you say Gloria and Peter were kind to you?"

"Is that Mr. Simms's name? Peter?"

"Yes. Pete Junior is the deputy." Millie stuffed popcorn into her mouth.

"They were amazing." Her mouth tilted up when she replayed the day. "I promised Wyatt I'd go with him tomorrow night to the Rose & Thorn."

Millie's brows shot up. "The alehouse? That's not your kind of place."

Shrugging, Olivia reached into the bowl for another handful of the salty snack they shared most nights before bed. "It's not, but Wyatt hangs out with his friends there, and they are planning a birthday party for him."

"I see."

"You look like you disapprove."

"I'm worried. You're ready to face the Uniform Chasers at the Rose & Thorn. It's not what it once was since those young women have taken it over."

"Uniform Chasers?" Olivia frowned.

"Women who are after a man in uniform. It's a status thing, Liv."

"Oh."

"You're nothing like them, dear, and I'm sure Wyatt appreciates that. I know his mother does."

"Do you know Mrs. Simms?"

"It's a tiny town."

"Are you friends?"

"We're friendly." She pointed the remote at the screen. "Are you ready for another episode?"

"First, do you have any advice for me?"

"Advice?"

"About tomorrow night. I've seen some of the women you mentioned, and they don't seem...friendly." And wasn't the Rose & Thorn Joey's hangout? Dread washed over her. "I want to fit in, or at least not stand out."

"You don't want to fit in with their sort. Trust me." Millie's lips pressed together. "Just be yourself, Liv. That's why Wyatt likes you."

"I want to look good."

"It wouldn't hurt to get a new outfit and try a bit of lippy."

"I wouldn't even know where to start with clothes."

Millie turned to her. "My friend Gayle is a stylist at the

Desert Rose boutique. If you're serious about a new look, head in and tell her I sent you. She'll take good care of you."

"A new look." Olivia rolled the idea around. Maybe she needed to do more than ditch her glasses. "I'd hoped to have my contact lenses by now."

Millie patted her hand. "Even though the shipment was delayed, you can still make a little change and show off the best version of yourself."

"I don't know what that looks like."

"The Bible says not to throw away your confidence."

"I'm not sure that verse isn't out of context in this situation."

Millie shrugged one shoulder and stirred the unpopped kernels around the bottom of the bowl. "Just be yourself only with a drop of glam."

"Glam?"

"Some color. It doesn't hurt to try something new, Liv. The same old you with a new coat of paint."

A new coat of paint? She wasn't a car, for goodness sake. Still...

*W*yatt's friends were going to roast him. Matching with Olivia was one thing—and they'd badger him plenty about that—but wearing matching sweaters with his dog? He might as well hand his man card over. Joey would flay him, and he'd deserve it. Trading his dignity for the affection of a pretty girl? He should know better at his age.

First responders developed thick skins to survive their jobs, but Olivia wasn't a first responder, and the inevitable jokes tonight would probably be hurtful to someone as sweet and sensitive as Olivia. He needed to convince her not to take them personally.

The party would test Olivia's grit, but if they had a future together, Olivia needed to know upfront that a relationship with a firefighter required a fair amount of toughness. Firefighters were sometimes a bit rough around the edges.

Wyatt peered at his reflection in the mirror. Stormy gray eyes looked back, clouded with conflict. The sweater was fine on its own, but it would cause a ruckus at the party paired with Olivia's matching one.

He heaved a sigh, shoved his wallet into his pocket, and grabbed his keys on the way out the door. At the last minute, he decided to leave Steve behind. "Stay home, buddy."

Olivia had been excited to learn that the Rose & Thorn allowed leashed dogs in the outside seating area. Steve might have helped her relax, but Steve in a sweater—especially a matchy sweater? No way.

Wyatt drove under the speed limit to Millie's. A sense of impending doom made his gut churn.

Olivia's green VW Bug sat next to Millie's Mercedes in the driveway of the bungalow-style house. There wasn't room for another vehicle, so he parked on the roadside. He sat in the cab with his eyes closed and took a few deep breaths. Who needed a birthday party at thirty-two anyway? They could have had a quiet dinner together at El Cibo. But his friends had gone to a lot of trouble. Besides, skipping out on his party wouldn't endear Olivia to his friends. He said a little prayer inside the cab before he jumped out and forced himself up the stairs to knock on the bright blue door.

The door swung open, and Millie swept him inside with her arm around his waist. "My, aren't you handsome in that sweater?"

Olivia appeared. "Hi, Wyatt." Her shy smile knocked his heart sideways. She wore a flowery skirt and boots with her olive green sweater. She'd curled her shiny brown hair and left it down instead of tucked up in her usual bun.

"You look pretty," he said when he found his breath.

"Doesn't she?" Millie beamed. "The both of you...so adorable in matching sweaters. Hold on one minute, let me snap a picture for your mothers."

Olivia pushed her glasses up on her nose. "Please, Aunt Millie—"

But Millie's hand was faster than the eye, and she'd taken a couple of shots before Wyatt could even smile in the camera's direction.

"Now, scoot closer, Liv, and show me some teeth. There, just like that. You too, Wyatt." She nodded, apparently satisfied, and dropped her phone into the folds of her housecoat. "I thought your dog was coming so the three of you could show off your matching outfits?" She tilted her head.

"Uh...Steve had a little stomach upset. I didn't think he should go on a drive. Didn't want him to, you know...in the truck."

"Oh, No. Of course not." She made a face and then waved them away. "Have fun, you two. And Wyatt, happy birthday."

"Thank you," he called over his shoulder. He hurried to catch Olivia, who'd bolted out the door.

She was buckled up with her cheeks the color of cabernet wine grapes before Wyatt reached the truck.

He chuckled. "Are you okay? It's not like she's interviewing us for the paper."

Olivia frowned and pushed her glasses up. "That's what you think. For all you know, she's alerted the Meddling Mama's grapevine, and you'll read a whole column about us in the morning. I'm sure at least one of those women is connected to the editor of the Wild Rose Observer."

Wyatt laughed. Humor released tension for him, but Olivia wasn't amused.

"Are you nervous about hanging out with my friends?"

Olivia gave a shuddery little nod.

Taking her into his arms and kissing her forehead gently was a tempting idea, but since he had no idea how she'd respond to that, he fired the engine instead. "It will be fine, you'll see." He gave her a tender smile.

Her pert little nose lifted, and she sent him a half-hearted smile.

People spilled out of the outer yard of The Rose & Thorn. The alehouse shook with music and shouting. Everyone Wyatt had ever known seemed to have shown up for his birthday party. Even his fourth-grade teacher held up a glass of ale. A live band played popular cover tunes for all they were worth, and the dancing was wild.

"So many…" Olivia pushed her glasses up and tugged her sweater down.

Wyatt took her hand and gave it a reassuring squeeze. "Everyone's going to love you." He'd almost said, *like I do,* but thank goodness that hadn't spilled out of his mouth. It was way too early for him to think about *that* word.

For the next hour, Wyatt didn't think much at all. He shook hands and introduced Olivia around. Then, the band began playing the birthday song, and someone pushed them upfront. The crowd hooted and jumped when Joey set a cake topped with blazing fireworks for candles in front of Wyatt. Olivia stepped sideways, but Wyatt reached for her hand. Hector shoved a burly guy out of his chair and invited Olivia to sit away from the spotlight.

Wyatt's friends began chanting. "Blow it out."

"Make a wish!"

"Put out the fire, fireman!"

Wyatt shot a glance at Olivia and lifted a questioning brow. She nodded, indicating that she was okay, so he went ahead and blew on the candles, knowing they would only blaze higher. They'd used the same kind for one of the medics last year.

Sparks flew, and everyone cheered Wyatt. He smiled and high-fived until the crowd around the cake thinned, and he spotted Olivia. Hector, bless him, stood beside her chair like a bodyguard.

Wyatt slipped away from his well-wishers and clapped Hector on the back. "Thanks, man."

He took Olivia by the hand. "Liv, are you hungry? The food is over there." He pointed to the far side of the room. "Or," he ventured, "we could dance first?"

She just blinked. The band struck up a slow song, and Wyatt tugged her gently toward the dance floor. He wanted to hold Olivia, press her close, breathe her in until she relaxed in his arms.

They swayed together, and she softened.

Resting her head on his collarbone, she sighed.

Olivia fit underneath his chin perfectly. He closed his eyes, melting into the moment. He'd never felt this way about another woman. Once or twice, he'd felt strong attraction, maybe even more, but nothing this powerful and pure.

Olivia tightened her arms around his neck, and everyone around them disappeared. They might have been alone, enveloped in the music, and falling in love.

They jumped when the drummer went nuts, and the band started playing a fast song. Olivia disconnected herself and hurried off the dance floor like a startled deer. Wyatt trailed her to the edge of the floor, then became aware of shouts. A group of guys acting like gorillas were getting rowdy. He followed their eyes to Christine and some of her friends dancing in front of the band wearing skimpier-than-usual outfits.

Olivia crept up beside him.

Trish waved and blew a kiss in Wyatt's direction. "Come dance, birthday boy."

Olivia stiffened and stepped back into the shadows.

Time for a change of scenery. "I'm starved." He led Olivia toward the buffet table. "Let's eat outside where it's quieter."

He handed Olivia a plate and took another for himself. She nabbed forks and reached for the napkins when Eddie, a rookie known to drink too much, jostled her, making her drop her plate.

Wyatt gave Eddie a shove. "Watch it, man."

"Sorry," Eddie mumbled. He stepped back and took in Wyatt and Olivia's matching sweaters. Manufacturing an exaggerated look of interest, he pointed. "Did you make those yourself?"

Olivia hesitated, eyes guarded. "Yes."

He raised his eyebrows and looked at Olivia with a snake oil salesman smile. "Wow."

Wyatt stepped in Eddie's line of sight and warned him off with a glare. He turned to Olivia. "I'm sorry. The guy's a jerk."

A probationary firefighter, Tom Dotson, interrupted the scene when he got in the food line with his girlfriend. As the petite redhead scooped baked beans, Tom dug into the pile of fried chicken. "Happy birthday, Wyatt."

"Thanks." Wyatt acknowledged Tom and moved past the pizza in favor of the cake. Olivia came alongside, and Wyatt cut another slice.

Tom and his date passed Olivia and Wyatt to the salad section.

Tom caught his girlfriend's gaze with wide eyes. "Please, don't ever do that to me," he spoke out of the side of his mouth.

Olivia froze, and the cake fell to the floor. Tom's girlfriend gave her a sympathetic look and scowled at Tom.

"Come on, Liv," Wyatt spoke in a gentle tone.

She shook her head and made for the front door. By the time Wyatt found a table to set their plates on, she'd vanished.

# 8

## DRAGONFLIES AND GRAPES

*O*livia wouldn't cry, not in a public place. Wyatt's voice reached her above the music, calling her name, but she pretended not to hear him and walked faster. When she chanced a peek over her shoulder, their eyes met, so she dodged a cluster of women and slipped into the ladies' bathroom.

There was a line. Of course, there was a line. What did she think? A bar this crowded wasn't going to have a mile-long wait for the toilets and mirrors? All she needed was a safe place to get ahold of herself but this wasn't it. She pivoted around and rushed out the heavy, wooden door into the brick wall of Wyatt's chest.

"Liv." Wyatt settled his hands on her shoulders.

"I need to get out of here," she sobbed. She hadn't meant to sound like that.

"If you want to go—and I get why you do—we'll go together."

"No." She pushed her glasses higher. "These people are here to celebrate your birthday."

"Nobody would even notice if I left." He gave her a slight smile. "They don't need a reason to party."

"They already think I'm a loser, I won't take you away from your birthday."

"I don't care about the party." He lifted her chin and searched her eyes. "I care about you."

Two women burst out of the bathroom door. They stopped short, took in Wyatt and Olivia's matching sweaters, and howled. They held on to one another, bumping into people and knocking over a pitcher of ale.

Olivia turned to Wyatt. "This isn't my kind of place or my kind of people." She pulled away from him and hurried to the door but found another line. She was trapped inside. Gulping air, trying to shake off claustrophobia, she spied another exit and pushed toward it.

Voices raised above the music carried and spurred her to move faster.

"That's Wyatt's new girlfriend?"

"Can you believe it?"

Tears burned Olivia's eyes and fogged her glasses. She didn't bother being considerate but shoved until she reached the parking lot. Bending at the waist to catch her breath, she remembered she hadn't driven herself.

She'd have to walk home.

She hated ruining Wyatt's night, but this felt like high school. What had she been thinking? The nerdy girl never got the cool guy. At least, not for long.

Footsteps pounded the blacktop behind her. "There you are." Wyatt panted.

Olivia winced but turned to face the man so clearly out of her league. "Go have fun with your friends."

"We came together, and we'll leave together. Besides, how were you planning on getting home?"

"I'm perfectly capable of walking, It's less than a mile."

Wyatt's jaw flexed. "I won't let you walk alone in the dark."

She gave him a sad smile. "Wyatt, I don't belong."

"I'll tell you what, let me bring our plates out here. We can eat at one of those tables." He pointed to three empty picnic tables underneath yellow lights. "I want to be wherever you are, Liv."

It had gone dark while they'd been inside, and the autumnal air chilled her. She rubbed goosebumps on her arms. "No, thanks, I'm serving coffee at church early in the morning. I should go." Releasing a sigh, she headed for Wyatt's truck. "Guess the sweaters weren't the big hit I thought they'd be."

Wyatt caught up and reached for her hand.

When she glanced sideways, she noticed his sheepish look. "You knew."

"I don't care what other people think."

Her wounded heart softened. "You're the nicest man." Olivia pulled her hand free of his. "And the handsomest. You can choose any woman you want. Why are you interested in me?"

"I like you." His gray eyes searched her face.

"I like you too, but is that enough?"

"I think so."

"We're so different." She clenched her eyes. "You're a firefighter. You guys build trauma bonds and become a kind of family I'll never be part of. I've read about it." Olivia didn't like to admit it, but after Mrs. Vick's comments at the shop, she'd researched.

Wyatt tipped his head. "The fire department isn't my whole life. Those guys are my friends, not my world."

"You're close with them." Olivia swept her arm over the Rose & Thorn. "They're cool and fun, and I'm...not."

"I think you're cool and fun."

Olivia rolled her eyes. "They'll never accept me."

"They're rowdy, but they're good people. Give them time."

"I know they're good people." Her cheeks heated with the old shame of being made fun of by her peers. She should be beyond these feelings, so why was she willing to give up the best thing that had ever happened because of a few hurtful words?

Wyatt took her hands and pressed them to his chest. "You're an amazing lady. Some day, they'll wise up and see what I see."

"You deserve someone more interesting than me, someone they would relate to better." She pulled her hands out of his and yanked at the neck of her sweater. "I make everyone uncomfortable. I always have."

"You're shy. The way you blush is one of the many reasons I can't get my mind off you," Wyatt's voice was melty, like warm honey on toast.

It would be easy to believe Wyatt and let herself fall for him. But echoes of her college boyfriend's voice whispered to her. "This relationship is dull, and you're....uninspiring, Olivia. I need someone who makes me feel alive." The relationship had been short-lived but had left a mark on her self-esteem like a permanent bruise.

Wyatt reached for her hands again, placing them over his heart. "They're still partying in their thirties. Who says that's cool?"

Olivia pulled her hands away from Wyatt's solid chest, immediately missing the warmth and sense of safety. But she should break things off with him before she got crushed like a bug again. Better to be alone than rejected. "Please, Wyatt, just take me back to Millie's." She headed for his truck.

Wyatt caught one of her hands and held it as he walked beside her, head down. "You're making a mistake, Liv. We like each other too much to give up so easily."

Giggling women piled out of a car beside the truck. They adjusted skirts, searched for phones, and checked mirrors. All of them were beautiful, smiling, and ready for a fun night.

"Hi, Wyatt. Why aren't you on the dance floor? Come on." A tall brunette slipped her arm under Wyatt's elbow. She turned to Olivia. "Let's make sure Wyatt's birthday is one he won't ever forget." She smiled and tugged at Olivia's sweater. "Nice."

A blonde with pink-dipped tips on the ends of her hair climbed out of the driver's side of the car. "Jessie, put my keys in your purse." She had long legs and high boots. "Betcha this is your new girlfriend, huh?" She winked and slammed the door. "Love the naughty librarian look."

Olivia gulped.

Pink Tips stuck her hand out. "I'm Terri."

"Wyatt's told us about you," a petite woman said. Her eyes sparkled when they darted toward the party. The band played a popular fast song, and her bounces and hops suggested she was ready to dance.

"It's nice to meet you." Olivia's face flamed hotter by the second. She'd give anything to be carefree and friendly like these girls, but she wasn't, and she couldn't fake it.

What would it be like to be part of a friend group? Olivia had been an outcast at school, eating lunch alone. Her adult life hadn't proved much better. Maybe that's why she was drawn to elderly people. They were often lonely. However, the Birding Betties were like these girls, only wrinkled, and they loved her.

Terri squealed and clapped. "A cover band, how fun!"

"Let's request…" Their voices died away as they skipped in a huddle toward the back gate.

Opening the passenger side door for her, Wyatt waited until Olivia belted in before he went around to the driver's side. He started the engine and turned to face her. "I'm sorry."

"No need." She sounded prim. Why did she do that? Why not toss her hair and flirt? Why had she never learned to dance?

"Steve and I will see you Thursday for knitting class."

Olivia's eyes widened. "You're still coming? After tonight's fiasco, I thought—"

"I'm more resilient than you give me credit for, Liv."

Turning her face aside, she bit her bottom lip. She'd made a fool out of herself. Why couldn't she have just laughed off the insults and decided to enjoy herself instead of running out like a coward—and worse—making Wyatt leave his party to follow her?

"You can still go back," she said in a small voice.

But Wyatt shook his head. "I don't want to hang out with people who hurt you."

"It's my fault. I'm too shy. It's always been a problem."

Pulling to a stop in front of Millie's home, Wyatt faced her. "If you think I'm giving up on you that easily, Olivia, you don't know me yet."

Something inside Olivia swelled. Didn't every woman want a man to pursue her and fight dragons to save her? Even if those dragons were of her own making?

Mom might make fun of romance novels, but she'd never met a hero like Wyatt Simms.

*W*yatt studied his sister with amusement from underneath half-closed eyes. He and Hazel had worked hard picking grapes all morning and were enjoying a break.

A blue dragonfly landed on the tip of Hazel's nose as she lay supine under the shade of an apple tree. Her eyes fixed on the creature then crossed.

Wyatt sat with his back against the tree trunk, arms behind his head, and legs stretched out.

"Do they sting?" Hazel whispered.

"I have no idea."

"Lotta help you are," she whispered.

He leaned over, arm outstretched to shoo the dragonfly away.

"Don't."

"Are you trying to get stung?"

"They aren't bees."

Steve jumped up and snuffled Hazel's face, and growled.

With a whirring like a helicopter, the blue dragonfly lifted off Hazel's freckled nose and flew away. She sat up with a frown.

"Steve, you made it fly away," she scolded.

The dog skulked back to the shady spot where he liked to keep a watchful—if dozing—eye on them.

Wyatt cocked his head. "Do you think I'm a nice guy?"

"Depends."

"On what?"

"Who you're hanging out with."

He raised his brows.

"When you're around a bunch of firefighters, you can be an idiot."

He served her a mock glower. "Don't hold back or anything."

"Why are you asking me?" She pulled a dried twig from her curls.

"You're my little sister. You'll tell the truth. Pete would say something jerky. Mom would tell me I'm an angel, and I'd never ask Dad that question."

Hazel sat cross-legged and looked up with a sly smile. "Why not ask Olivia?"

His shoulders dipped. "I'm afraid I know what she'd say."

"You don't look too happy about it."

"The guys threw me a party at the Rose & Thorn. Everybody showed, and I was excited to bring Olivia, but then she wanted us to—"

"Wear those matching sweaters." She grimaced. "Yeah. They're bad."

"Olivia's sweet for making them." Wyatt stiffened in defense.

"Sure, but matching with your girlfriend is a dork move."

"Let's just say it made an impression."

"Not in a positive way, I'll bet."

"A few of the women got snotty about it. One of the guys made fun of Olivia, and she got her feelings hurt."

"What did you do?"

"I took her home like she wanted."

"You didn't stick up for her?" Hazel's eyes frosted. "She's different, but she's cool in her own way. We all like her, so don't go getting us all hurt again, Wyatt."

Wincing, he pictured Lynette's back the last time he saw her walking away. They'd dated for over a year before she finally got fed up with the everlasting firefighter frat party wherever the Wild Rose Fire Department crew gathered. Not everyone, but most of that group were Wyatt's closest friends, and even he had to admit they went too far sometimes.

"Yes, I'm talking about Lynette. Mom and Dad loved her, and I thought she'd become my big sister."

Tossing a pebble at a grasshopper, Wyatt sighed. "Sorry, Hazie."

Hazel scooted closer and met Wyatt's eyes. "You can't do that to us again."

"Wasn't fun for me either."

"If you want a happily-ever-after, brother, you can't pretend to be twenty-one forever. It's time to grow up, even if your friends don't." She crossed her arms. "Good luck finding a worthy woman who wants to be part of this family, not just a party girl who thinks it's enough to decorate your arm."

He frowned. "You think I'm looking for marriage?"

"Don't try to be cute, Wy. You and I both know that's why you brought Olivia to meet us."

He hadn't considered his reasons for introducing Olivia to his family so soon. He was crazy about her and, on impulse, had shared his home and family with her. Or maybe he'd wanted to share her with them. Either way, he and Olivia clicked, like something missing fell into place, and he wanted her to be in every corner of his life.

He glanced up to find Hazel's gaze trained on him. He knew her too well. She was waiting for him to deny her words.

"You might be right." He shrugged one shoulder. "I don't know. I just…I like her and wanted all of you to like her too."

Hazel's eyes softened. "What did Olivia think of us?"

"She said she liked you all a lot."

"Even Pete?"

"If you can believe it."

"That settles it. Olivia's a keeper. If she can put up with you, your buddies, *and* Pete, then she's the clear choice."

Wyatt laughed. "There's no one else to choose from anyway."

"Not true." Hazel leaned back on her elbows. "Half of the single women in town and plenty of tourists look at you like they could gobble you up. You could date lots of other women." She lifted her face to the noon sun. "But you like Olivia."

"I'm not so sure she likes me as much. She keeps saying we aren't right for each other."

"So, prove her wrong."

"How?"

"You're a smart guy, so don't act dumb."

"I'm insulted."

"No, you're not. You already know what you have to do. You just don't want to do it."

"Little Miss Know-It-All today, huh?"

"You're the one who asked. I was trying to have a nap before the next row."

"Huh. Speaking of the next row, we better get back to work. We have four more before we can quit for the day."

Hazel stood and stretched. She dusted the dirt and dried grape leaves from her behind. "Are you coming to watch the movie production crew with us tonight?"

"Why would I do that?"

"Pete's on standby."

"I'm going to knitting class tonight."

"I can't believe you said that with a straight face." Snickering, she jumped away from his playful swat. "Next thing we know, you'll join the Meddling Mamas who only pretend to knit stuff for charity in that shop. They don't have anyone fooled."

Wyatt curled his lip. "Keep it up, and I'll remind them you're twenty-five and still unmarried."

He laughed as his petite sister lunged for him. "Don't you dare!"

Steve bounced between them and began barking. He loved a play fight. Wyatt tapped his leg to summon Steve and ran for the vineyard. The vines hung heavy with juicy grapes, and their perfume hung in the air.

Hazel's head popped up from the other side of the row, and Steve gave a joyful bark before shooting underneath the vine frame to join her. She stuck her tongue out. "Nah. See, Steve's on my side."

"Stealing my dog is just putting another nail in your coffin... I'll drop your single status for sure next time I'm at Hooked On Ewe."

She nailed him with a fistful of rotten grapes.

"Ouch." Wyatt wiped sticky gunk from his eye.

"If you do, I'll tell Olivia you wet the bed until you were twelve."

"I did not."

Hazel volleyed a wicked smile over the vine. "It's my word against yours, big brother."

"You wouldn't." He laughed.

"Oh, wouldn't I?"

"Then I'll have no choice but to tell Dad you're the one who ran over his toolbox with the tractor."

Hazel's eyes widened. "You promised."

"You're playing dirty, I'm only defending myself."

"Ha."

Finding an overripe bunch of grapes close to hand, Wyatt fingered them, weighing his options. He plucked them and lifted his arm, intending to pelt Hazel when Dad came around the corner, whistling. He strolled past with a full pail in each hand. Hazel and Wyatt's eyes met over the vines, and Hazel clapped a hand over her mouth to quiet her laughter.

"Are you two ever going to grow up?" Dad used his long-suffering voice from over his shoulder.

Straightening, Wyatt began to clip clusters of warm, plump grapes and set them in the containers at his feet.

"Bet I can finish with more boxes than you," Hazel challenged.

Unable to leave that alone, he doubled his efforts.

An hour later, they were sticky and exhausted, but they high-fived on the way to separate bathrooms. Wyatt had won, naturally, but suspected Hazel had used Mom's trick of motivating him to pick more fruit in a way she knew he couldn't refuse. He peeled off his sweat-stained shirt.

He and Steve were going to meet Olivia for a late lunch in the park. He'd managed to persuade her that Steve missed her and mentioned that the Bow Wow Bakery had a sidewalk sale, knowing full well Olivia couldn't resist buying Steve's favorite treats.

He whistled on his way to the shower.

## 9

## THE SHEEP FARM

owering her binoculars, Olivia settled on them on the park bench beside Wyatt. "I think you're right, it's just a duck, not the lake monster." She turned to grin at him, and a warm flush washed over her when he smiled back.

"Don't feel bad. Steve thought it was the monster, too." Wyatt set aside the sweater they'd worked on for the past two weeks.

Steve lifted his head from the top of his paws when he heard his name.

Wyatt's gray eyes reflected the lake in front of them with blue flecks. He was handsome in a white T-shirt underneath a green and charcoal flannel. There was a little hole in the knee of his jeans, which made her smile. Wyatt seemed just as confident in old jeans as in his dark blue Wild Rose Fire and Rescue uniform.

A cluster of dark clouds hovered over the water, but since they were under the shelter of dogwood trees, she wasn't worried about their picnic being spoiled. Olivia's lunch hour had become her favorite part of the day because, for the past few weeks, Wyatt and Steve either met her in the park or Wyatt treated her to a meal at Frog Legs Bar & Grill. They'd become close, maybe even a couple.

Olivia fished around inside the Bow Wow Bakery bag for a dog cookie. She raised a questioning brow in Wyatt's direction, asking his permission. Wyatt smiled and nodded. Steve's snack radar went off at the sound of rustling paper, and he sat up.

"Who's a good boy? That's my Stevie." She laid the cookie in her palm and let Steve take it from her hand.

"He's getting fat." Wyatt turned to face her. "You know someone's making a movie downtown. There are sign-up sheets for people who'd like to be extras on set."

"The Legend And His Love. Millie had me tack up flyers in the window." Olivia pulled out a sandwich, offered it to Wyatt, and then rooted out another for herself. "Are you thinking of signing up? I can see you doing something like that."

"Only if you'll do it with me." Wyatt unwrapped his ham and cheese and took a huge bite.

"Not a chance." She shuddered.

"Rumor is lots of locals have signed up."

Wyatt's handsome face belonged on a screen. But she was too shy, too plain, and too...herself. "You should do it," she said around a delicate bite. She baked homemade bread for today's sandwiches last night.

Wyatt shook his head. "Not without my girl." He tore another bite out of his sandwich.

She snuck a glance out of the corner of her eye. Wyatt was dreamy, even when he was savaging his lunch. She'd never known anyone who could eat as much as Wyatt. Except Steve. "I was thinking I'd like to buy tickets for the rodeo on the thirteenth of next month." She snuck another peek to see his reaction.

"I love a good rodeo. How about I get the tickets when I stop in at the feedstore for my mom's chicken food?" He looked like a young boy when he shrugged. "She gives me to-do lists."

"I don't mind paying." Olivia bit into an apple.

Wyatt gave her a sly grin. "Do I have to start wearing a cowboy hat and boots to win your heart?"

With a chunk of apple lodged in her throat, Olivia croaked an unintelligible answer.

Wyatt pounded her back. "Hey, I was just kidding. It's okay if you have a thing for the Cowboys. Most women do."

Olivia struggled to catch her breath after spewing apples on the ground at their feet. Wyatt handed her a napkin from their insulated bag along with a water bottle.

"Sorry, Liv. I was only kidding." The concern in his tone soothed her irritation.

Olivia wiped her eyes and put her glasses back on. She should be used to Wyatt's jokes and playfulness. "Do you always just blurt out whatever you think?"

"Bad habit."

"I don't want to go to ogle the cowboys," she said in her librarian voice. "Rodeo is a professional sport."

The squeal of a child interrupted their conversation.

"Hi, guys. Love that color on you, Olivia." Nina Sutherland adjusted her toddler's stroller shade. "My aunt told me Olivia was teaching you to knit, Wyatt. I think it's so cool. I wish Sloan would try, I've heard it's a great stress reliever." She let Steve snuffle her toddler, who took the opportunity to pull the dog's ears. Steve didn't seem to mind.

"I'm *crocheting* this gorgeous sweater, not knitting." Wyatt arched his brow.

They bantered while Nina and Sloan's child giggled at Steve. If only Olivia could be as confident and easy talking with people as beautiful Nina and charming Wyatt. She was like a wilted weed next to two roses.

Nina leaned over for a closer look at Wyatt's project. She fingered the stitches and raised her eyes to Olivia. "I'm impressed. I wish I could get knitwear of this quality into the boutique, but the cost..." she drifted off. "Anyway, I've got to go. We're meeting Sloan at Frog Legs."

Wyatt tickled the child's bare toes. "Seems you've lost your shoes, little one." He looked up. "Frog Legs is our place, right, Liv?" He turned a Crest-worthy smile on Olivia, the one that never failed to make her heart bash into her ribs.

Olivia gathered the ball of yarn the toddler had swatted to the ground before it could roll under the bench. "The grilled cheese is perfection."

"I'm a fan of the double bacon burger and onion rings." The lean blonde winked and continued down the sidewalk.

Olivia sighed. "Nina's so pretty."

Rummaging for another sandwich and finding it— Olivia always packed him two—Wyatt turned a narrowed eye on her. "You're not jealous of Nina Sutherland?"

"No. But I'd give anything for half of Nina's beauty and confidence. She must be smart, too, since she runs her own business." Olivia dropped her gaze to the rust-colored sweater she'd chosen this morning. Next to Nina's stylish jeans and charcoal cashmere hoody, Olivia resembled someone's granny. Now that she thought about it, even the Birding Betties dressed better than she did.

Wyatt set his sandwich down and scooped up Olivia's hands. "I'd bet my Christmas bonus that when Nina sees you, she wishes she had eyes half as pretty as yours."

Her cheeks heated like they always did when Wyatt complimented her. "I admit I'm a little…insecure, but that's my problem, not Nina's. She's sweet and funny, and I like her."

"You're all of those things, too." He dropped her hands and pointed. "Now, about the sweater. I love it, the color makes your eyes pop, and even though I like the green one better, I'd totally wear one just like it if you made it."

She couldn't help but laugh. Wyatt was too good to be true.

She picked up his half-finished sweater. The yarn was a shade of dove gray. He meant to finish it for his sister before Christmas but wasn't making much progress. Sometimes, it even looked like a row or two had unraveled.

Steve stood and nosed the treat bag.

"That's enough, buddy." Wyatt tossed a ball, and Steve lunged after it. "Don't chase the ducks, Steve."

"Is your mom singing at church tomorrow?" Mrs. Simms had a beautiful voice. Wyatt's family included her in their inner circle at church, and the sense of belonging warmed her. Now that Wyatt attended whenever his shifts allowed, Olivia and Millie sat with the Simms family on Sunday mornings.

"I was hoping she had a solo again."

"Nope. All hands on deck for harvesting grapes. Speaking of harvest, I'll be in the vineyards all next week when I'm not on shift at the fire station." He met her eyes. "Will you miss me?"

He was incorrigible but also…adorable. Olivia managed a nod. She was getting more comfortable with him every day.

An elderly couple leading a Chihuahua wearing a bright red dog coat passed by.

Olivia caught a napkin blown in the lake breeze. "I

wonder if I should knit another sweater for Steve. I can't believe he lost his."

Wyatt resumed eating with his eyes down.

"I forgot to ask if you'd mind taking me to Swenson's sheep farm again. I've driven there twice, but nobody will answer the door."

"I've been worried about Mr. Swensen and asked if someone to do a welfare check on him." He took his phone out. "I'm sorry I should have followed up, I'll ask Lieutenant Moore if anyone's gone yet." He thumbed a text.

"Millie said he doesn't have any relatives."

"None that we know of. He never married. Mom and Dad usually look in once in a while, but during harvest season, they're too busy."

A ping sounded from Wyatt's phone. "Hmmm." He frowned.

"What is it?" Olivia placed her hand on his arm.

"Mr. Swensen's recovering from a fall. He didn't get up to answer the door, so the crew went through a window to check on him, which scared him out of his wits. They found him in his chair in front of the television." He fixed her with a soft look. "Sounds like he could do with a little home cooking and a visit from friends."

"Why didn't anybody realize he'd been hurt and was alone?"

"He's always kept to himself."

"I should take him a meal. I'll talk to Millie. I'm sure she'll be happy to bake him a pie."

"I'll go with you," Wyatt offered.

They made plans to deliver a meal to Mr. Swensen and see if they could help in any other way.

Olivia glanced at her watch. She was late getting back to

the shop. "See you tonight." She patted Steve and gave Wyatt a smile that hopefully conveyed some little bit of the big things she felt for him.

Wyatt Simms was the best man she'd ever met. Not only was he a brave firefighter, a hard worker, and a loyal friend, but now she also knew he was a concerned neighbor.

*W*yatt guided Olivia through the overgrown path that led to Mr. Swensen's front door. He carried a casserole dish containing a ham and potato dish by its handle. Olivia armed herself with a tin of sugar cookies just in case the old man needed sweetening. Millie claimed that Mr. Swenson was a rascal and she'd burned the pie, so...

Olivia stumbled, and Wyatt shot out a hand to catch her. "Careful, those roses have thorns."

Olivia bent down to examine a tear in her skirt. "They sure do." It was a small snag. She straightened and turned sideways through the rest of the bushes, overtaking the path and porch.

"I think I'll get Dad and Pete to come back with me tomorrow to mow the grass and cut these bushes back. No wonder poor Mr. Swensen fell."

"He knows we're coming, right?" The anxiety in her voice made him slow his steps.

"My Mom called to let him know. He was happy to hear dinner's on the way."

Once Olivia was safely up the porch steps, he took the chance to orient himself to the place. He hadn't been here since before the Fire Academy. The land was pretty flat and overgrown with evergreen trees. A small apple orchard cried out for attention, and a blackberry patch had taken hostage a formerly beautiful peach grove. A pond to the right of the house peeked out from behind water weeds. In his youth, Mr. Swensen stocked it with trout and allowed them to fish it after they helped with the twice-yearly sheep shearing. Wyatt's gaze landed on the big rock. He and his siblings used to perch there, holding their poles in one hand and a bologna sandwich in the other. Mr. Swensen, the bologna king, kept them fed.

He smiled at the memories Swensen's farm conjured until he noticed the white fence surrounding the pond and pasture was falling down in several places. He'd bring his tools next time and ask Dad if he could spare extra lumber.

Olivia pointed to the far corner of the long porch. Along the side of the house sat a pile of squat, black garbage bags with curls of sheep fleece sticking out from the tops.

Wyatt rapped on the door. "Those must be Millie's bags of wool."

Scratches scarred the heavy wooden door near the middle. Wyatt craned his head to search through the tall grass and rose briars. "I wonder if he still has dogs." He knocked again and pressed his ear to the door.

Olivia peered into the dirty window on the side of the door. "I don't see anyone in the living room." She rubbed a spot with her elbow. "He doesn't have anyone?"

Shrugging one shoulder, Wyatt gave her an I-have-no-idea look. "I'll ask Pappy Rosmund about Mr. Swensen next time I'm on a call at Sunny Days Retirement Home. He's the oldest person on the Ridge and knows everything about everyone." He went to the retirement home several times a month.

"Let's find a way in." Olivia's wide-eyed worry for a man she didn't know warmed Wyatt's heart.

They found an unlocked side door—not very safe—and crept inside the dank, gloomy house. Wyatt lead the way down the hall and into the dirty kitchen. "Swensen could use a housekeeper." He kept his voice low.

Olivia pinched her nose.

They searched the main floor and, finding it empty, crept up the stairs.

"Do you hear that?" Olivia resembled a small mouse, frightened and clutching the cookies to her chest like a shield.

"Snoring." Wyatt grinned. This wasn't his first time searching a house for an older adult someone was worried about. "He's made it up to his bedroom somehow."

The open door of the first room at the top of the stairs was strewn with old Western paperback novels, socks, boxer shorts, and a stack of dirty plates. There, propped up in the middle of an old brass bed, lay Mr. Swensen. He snored so loudly that when Wyatt tiptoed closer, he expected to find the man's nose hair billowing from his nostrils.

He shook the bed slightly. "Mr. Swensen."

"Snort. Snort."

"It's Wyatt Simms. I have a friend with me. We brought you ham and potatoes in cheese sauce." He used his most persuasive voice.

Mr. Swensen's eyelids fluttered, and his mouth opened in a cavernous yawn.

Olivia backed into the doorway. She looked ready to bolt.

Smacking his lips, Mr. Swensen wrestled with the blankets and sat up. "Ouch."

Wyatt smiled to reassure Olivia and then turned to Mr. Swensen. "It's Wyatt, Mr. Swensen. Do you remember me?"

"Of course, I remember you." His furry brows drew together as his eyes focused on Olivia. "Who's that?"

Olivia shrunk back and held the cookies out to Wyatt.

"Mr. Swensen, meet Olivia Lewis, Millicent Rutherford's niece."

Olivia stepped toward the bed. "Nice to meet you, sir."

"Millie mentioned you. I'd forgotten you were coming, and as you can see, I'm not at my best. Downright undignified this is. You've caught me at a bad time."

Wyatt gave the man a once over, but he couldn't see much under the bed covers. "How did you manage the stairs, sir? I heard you'd taken a fall."

The old man's eyes narrowed. "I'm injured, not crippled." He passed gass. "Help me up, eh? I'm hungry as a bear coming out of hibernation in springtime." He threw off the covers to reveal raggedy boxers and a stained undershirt that might have been white at one time.

Olivia retreated into the hallway. "I'll wait downstairs."

"Darn tootin'." Mr. Swensen waved her away.

Wyatt helped him stand. He gave a low whistle after getting an eyeful of the man's bruises. "Man alive. How'd you manage that?" His bottom half was covered in fading purple, greens, and blues turning yellow. "These look over a week old."

Squinting at the calendar hanging precariously from a nail in the wall, Mr. Swensen touched a spot on his thigh that resembled soft, rotting fruit. "Two weeks."

"Those look painful. Let's get you dressed and presentable for company." Once Wyatt helped Mr. Swensen down the stairs and into his easy chair, Olivia brought him a dinner tray.

"I washed a few dishes. I hope you don't mind the intrusion; I couldn't find any clean ones when I was in the kitchen." She pushed her glasses up on her nose. "Understandable, considering."

"Thanks. Did you find the coffee pot by any chance?" Mr. Swensen had eyes only for his dinner and began to stuff his mouth. Who knew how long it had been since he'd eaten a decent meal? "Millie's a good cook," he said around a large bite.

Wyatt sat on the old sofa, trying to sink in on itself across from Mr. Swensen while Olivia rummaged in the kitchen. In short order, the old man sat sipping a cup of Folgers with an expression of pure contentment.

Wyatt let his gaze travel the room in a meaningful way. "You need a housekeeper. Has anyone come around to check on you since the fire department crew?"

"No, and it's been lonesome since Roy died."

Roy must have been his last dog. Mr. Swensen always had a dog or two. "You don't have a dog anymore?"

"Coyotes got Bertie and Roy passed right there on the couch of old age."

Wyatt jumped up and over to the worn, gold velvet chair next to the sofa. "How've you been getting along?"

The old timer sipped from his mug. "Not too good."

Olivia came from the kitchen with her hair pulled back, her sleeves up, and her face smudged. She'd tackled the mess while the older man ate and gone up about fifty more notches in Wyatt's estimation. Not many women would do what she'd done.

She collapsed into the dip in the sofa, and Wyatt opened his mouth to tell her about old Roy, but she'd probably suffered enough discomfort for one day. Besides, what she didn't know wouldn't hurt her. He'd remember to suggest she had a shower when she got home.

Mr. Swensen eyed her. "Thank you, young lady. What was your name again?"

"Olivia."

"That's right."

"I came here a couple of times to pick up the bags of fleece from your sheep, but you didn't answer the door, and we got worried, so—"

"Had a run of bad luck."

Wyatt leaned forward and prayed that he wouldn't poke holes in the man's pride. "It seems the place is getting a little beyond you."

"It is. That's a fact. I ran some ads in the Wild Rose Observer for a lodger or even just some day-help 'round the farm, but the only person who answered was a skinny woman who took one look around and skedaddled."

"You mean you searched for a housekeeper?" Wyatt asked.

Mr. Swensen shrugged. "Before the accident."

"Where are the sheep?" Olivia asked.

"Behind the shed. My neighbor's been feeding 'em, but that can't last forever."

"I like sheep." Olivia's cheeks turned the color of plums. "I'm willing to come out and help you."

Mr. Swensen set his coffee aside. "You will?"

"Yes."

Olivia might like sheep, but to Wyatt's knowledge, she'd never cared for them. He turned to Mr. Swensen. "Olivia works full-time in town, but she and I could help around here until you find a more permanent solution." Of course, he worked twenty-four-hour shifts besides nearly full-time in his family's vineyards.

Olivia leaned forward. "I'd love to come as often as possible."

What Mr. Swensen needed most was to sell this place and retire from sheep farming altogether. Giving the man false hopes would only prolong the inevitable.

Wyatt closed his eyes and refrained from shaking his head when Olivia wrote her cell number down on a notepad she'd found underneath a pile of old newspapers. Somehow, he'd have to convince her that Mr. Swensen needed more than she could give him.

## 10

## THE SHEEP FARMER

Olivia tossed another armful of alfalfa over the fence for Mr. Swensen's sheep. She'd been coming for two weeks even though Wyatt had tried to talk her out of it.

"Helping out Mr. Swensen makes me happy." She smiled up into the calico blue sky. Half a dozen ewes stood at the fence munching orchard grass. Olivia laughed as they jostled one another. A particularly large ewe with one black spot on her side butted another out of "her" pile.

She'd struck a bargain with the geriatric farmer. She'd care for the sheep as long as he promised to accept Meals On Wheels and hire a housekeeper. According to Millie, he had loads of money, so the sad state he'd gotten himself into was his own doing. At least, that's what she said while waving a wooden spoon in the air. She might complain about a person, but she wasn't one to let someone suffer on her watch. In short order, Mr. Swensen's freezer sparkled. Millie stuffed it with cookies and organized a supper train to get him through until his meal deliveries began.

The knitting club loaded cleaning supplies into Millie's work van and drove to the farm as soon as news of injuries spread. Together, they gave Mr. Swensen's house a thorough scrubbing. Millie's friend Ruthie Rosmund put herself in charge of interviewing housekeepers. She found one trustworthy and brave enough to get along with the temperamental elderly gentleman. Millie was satisfied that he was well looked after, but there was still the matter of his flock.

"The best way to help Mr. Swensen in selling his flock," Wyatt insisted when they'd discussed ways to assist. "Since he has difficulty caring for them properly, it's the right thing to do for the animals."

But the farmer became red in the face and flat refused. "I lost my dogs, I won't be deprived of my sheep, too!"

Wyatt's family took an afternoon off from their busy wine grape harvest to fix fences and administer overdue vaccinations to the flock. Olivia helped Wyatt give the ewes and ram doses of a nasty, white liquid he said would kill any internal worms, and then Pete trimmed their hooves. Olivia had smiled all day but showered when she got home and fell into bed.

A warm, wet nose pushed at her hand through the fence, snapping Olivia back into the moment. She looked down to find a small, spotted ewe. "Sorry, no more treats today." She held the hose over the sheep's water trough and let the peace of the farm and the company of the animals soak into her soul along with the autumnal warmth. Days like this were everything she dreamed about.

The sheep weren't hers, but that didn't stop her from falling madly in love with them. Once she'd filled the water trough, she put the hose away and opened the gate to spend some time with her favorites. The ewes were kept apart from the ram except during the autumn breeding season. Since Mr. Swensen agreed they shouldn't be bred this year, they could all be driven to the large pasture when Mr. Simms finished the grape harvest and had time to help.

But without the protection of dogs around, the sheep would be in danger from cougars and coyotes. There was a lot more to keeping a flock than Olivia ever imagined, yet she enjoyed learning everything she could about them and their care.

One of the ewes was braver than the rest. Olivia called her Betsy because she sported a funny cap of wool on her head, a shade different from the rest of her. "You remind me of the photo I saw of Betsy Ross," she said. The creature only snuffled Olivia's pockets, looking for more grain. When she stopped scratching Betsy so she could take some photos, she pawed her with sharp, newly cut hooves. "You're just like Steve when he wants more attention."

Her phone pinged with a text message, startling the ewe. She ran to the back of the flock, stamped her front foot, and watched Olivia with wary eyes.

"I'm sorry, it's just Millie. She wants me to stop at Nina's boutique to pick up a tote bag for her." Standing, Olivia dusted the hay and dirt off her clothes the best she could before leaving the sheep secured behind the newly repaired gate. As she got into her little VW Bug, she considered trading it for a small truck that would better fit her new life.

Olivia stopped at the eye clinic to get the contact lenses and stuffed the boxes into her purse. She drove to her next errand down the two-lane street bordered by golden, red, and yellow trees. She when she found a parking spot right in front of Nina's boutique.

When she stepped inside, a lush fragrance engulfed her in a drastic contrast to the sheep pen. Luxurious silk fabrics covered the windows. Nina, beautiful as always—how did she pull that off?—greeted her with a bright smile. "Millie told me to expect you. Feel free to browse while I search around in the back for her order. It came in a week ago, and I've lost track of it."

Olivia fingered a floral blouse. "It's no wonder, as full as your hands are with this place and a family to care for."

"I love it all," Nina called over her shoulder.

Voices carried in Olivia's direction from the back of the store. She pushed her glasses up to get a better view, but the lenses were smudged with sheep slobber. She took them off and cleaned them on the hem of her shirt.

"Look, Chris, isn't that Wyatt's little friend?" A woman from Wyatt's birthday party came closer than was polite. She thrust her hand at Olivia. "I'm Trish." Then, like an afterthought, she indicated the woman behind her. "This is Christine."

Olivia hesitated, unsure.

"So, how long have you and Wyatt been a thing?" The woman named Trish cocked her hip.

Disadvantaged by her poor eyesight, Olivia fumbled to get her glasses on. She pushed them higher and forced an unsure smile. "Hello, ladies." Well, that sounded matronly.

"So?" Christine prodded.

Olivia wasn't about to confide anything to this pair of Barracudas. How long she and Wyatt had been seeing one another was none of their business. "Excuse me." She tried to move past the wall of hair and lipgloss.

Both women moved to block her.

Trish bared a feral cat smile. She must consider Olivia, the mouse. "He'll get tired of you, you know." Her teeth were sharp and white and small.

What could Olivia say to that? And why should she bother? Trish was goading her. Everything Olivia knew about mean girls she'd learned in middle school: avoid them, and If that didn't work, ignore them. She pretended to be occupied with a display of earrings on her left side.

"Firefighters and cops are adrenaline junkies, babe. Wyatt loves the chase, but once he catches you..." Trish's eyebrows shot up.

Christine reached out and turned the display Olivia pretended to look at. "Well, Wyatt's a catch-and-release type of guy, isn't he?"

It wasn't really a question, so Olivia didn't bother trying to answer. Besides, she didn't think Wyatt was a love-them-and-leave-them guy. Did she?

Trish picked up a slinky dress and held it up. "All fire-fighters are the same, aren't they, Chris?"

"Yep. Firefighters love the challenge of someone new." Christine's cold eyes flitted over Olivia from head to toe and back again. She stepped closer.

Olivia backed up.

"Is that hay in your hair?" Christine's nose wrinkled in disgust.

"Probably," Olivia conceded.

"You don't get it, do you?"

Olivia sighed. They weren't going away. "Get what, Christine?"

"You're..."

"Average at best," Trish supplied.

Christine's face was a mask of false sympathy. "Wyatt's attention will wander, and when it does—"

"There you are." Nina carried a large bag in her hands and headed straight into their strange trio like a queen.

Olivia sagged with relief.

"There's a clearance rack in the back." Nina's smile was tight, her eyes cold. "You're on tight budgets if I remember."

The sneers fell off their faces and they stalked away like hyenas run off a kill by a lioness.

"Thanks," Olivia said.

Nina gave her a sympathetic smile and pulled the hay from Olivia's hair. "Sure. Those two are something, aren't they?"

"They're probably right, though."

"About?"

"Wyatt and me." Olivia pointed to the full-length mirror in front of them. "Wyatt's handsome, funny, cool, and I'm… not." She examined their images. She was a brown wren next to a bird of paradise. Nina, always polished, in style, and confident, put Olivia to shame.

"If I were more like you, women like them wouldn't bother me," Olivia said.

Nina met her eyes in the mirror. "I think you're wonderful just the way you are."

Tears filled Olivia's eyes, and she turned away from their reflections. "I'm tired of being me. I want to be…better."

"Does that mean you don't like yourself?"

The compassion in Nina's voice and her genuine curiosity gave Olivia the courage to be honest. She shook her head. "I don't know how I became *her*." She pointed to her reflection. "She's hiding the real me, and I want out."

"But you like who you are inside?" Nina's brows drew together.

"I don't know."

Looking concerned, Nina set down the bag. "Who do you want to be?"

Olivia shrugged one shoulder. "I only know who I *don't* want to be. The girl who never went to a single school dance." She stared at the dowdy woman in the mirror. How had she gotten so lost?

Nina frowned. "That makes me sad."

She didn't want Nina to feel sorry for her. Why'd she allow her to see what a loser she actually was?

Hooking her arm in Olivia's, Nina drew her close. "When I first came to Wild Rose Ridge, I met a guy I thought was homeless." She let go of Olivia's arm and grabbed her hand. "Let's sit over there." She indicated a white sofa underneath a crystal chandelier.

A fond smile stretched Nina's lips. "It was Sloan, my future husband, although I'd never guessed that then. Sloan was Bigfoot in Blue Jeans. No joke, the poor man went through the worst period of his life and came out of it a little ragged."

Olivia smiled politely.

"I needed a model, and my aunt Shirley promised me that Sloan Sutherland was a dreamboat underneath all that hair and dirt." She grinned. "He'd been working in the woods. We got him to the barber, and sure enough, he was gorgeous." She crossed her legs, flashing ankle boots that peeked out from flowy linen pants.

She turned light blue eyes on Olivia. "The point is that my husband was buried under who he'd become. His self-esteem tanked, and he was hiding from the world. Once he changed his outward appearance to match who he was inside, his confidence came back."

"So…if I change my look, I'll be more confident?" Olivia sometimes fantasized about making a radical change. If watching the original *Grease* forty-three times was any indication, pulling a Sandy to Wyatt's reformed bad boy Danny might work.

Placing a hand on Olivia's arm, Nina's expression softened. "Only if you think it would help you be the person you feel you are on the inside. My motto is look good, feel good, perform well."

"Will you help me?" The hope in Olivia's voice was a little desperate, even to her own ears.

But she *was* desperate.

A brilliant smile crossed Nina's face. "Consider me your fairy godmother. I know just the person to transform your pumpkin."

## 11

### GOING, GOING, GONE

*W*yatt backed the fire engine into the bay, flipped off the switch, and jumped down, smacking his boots on the cement floor. Joey landed with a thwack on the other side. Wyatt hung his helmet on its hook over his bunker gear and dragged a bucket to wash the rig while Joey power-washed.

Captain Vick burst through the door with his mouth in a grim line. "It's past eight. Your shift is over."

"Yessir." Joey stowed the hose as Vick crossed the bay.

Perpetually late for one meeting or another with the fire commissioners, the Captain wasn't one for small talk. "Drill starts in fifteen minutes, so you need to get out of our way, or we'll put you to work."

They jogged to the crew's living quarters and to their separate bedrooms. They needed showers after the ordeal of last night's accident. They'd been up all night, but none of the crew would have been able to sleep anyway.

Joey had been giving Wyatt the silent treatment for weeks, and Wyatt had been trying to think of a way to thaw the ice.

"Joey, want to ride over to Swensen's Sheep Farm after breakfast at Weavers Bakery?" A warm pastry and a massive mug of coffee sounded like a fix for what ailed them. It always worked in the past.

"What for?"

"I promised to repair the old man's steps before the week was out, and it sort of got away from me."

Joey's hand rasped against the stubble on his jaw. "Let me guess, Olivia's there?"

"Olivia's on a hike with the Birding Betties."

A grin cracked Joey's face. "The Birding Biddies?"

"Leave it alone," Wyatt gave him a good-natured warning.

Joey held up both hands. "Hey, who am I to judge? Birds are cool."

"Like I said, I'm going to fix Swensen's broken steps. I thought you'd like to come along since we don't see much of each other anymore."

"Yeah, sure. I've been meaning to check on old man Swensen anyway." Joey peeled off his soiled shirt. "Are you going to the carnival tomorrow?"

Snatching his towel and soap, Wyatt winced at the smell radiating from his uniform. He'd have to use the facilities at the station rather than take something contaminated home to wash in Mom's machine. "The rodeo, I guess." He shrugged. "Olivia might want to go to both."

"How about you?" He tipped his eyebrow.

"There's a kissing booth, so…"

"You have to pay for a kiss?"

"Nah, I'm kidding. There's a live band I want to listen to."

"Have a date?"

"I'm just going with the guys this time." He stalked down

the hall, wearing a towel around his waist. "Shower and meet me at your truck."

Wyatt showered, shaved, and dialed Olivia. It went straight to voicemail. "Hey, Liv. I just wanted to see if you're interested in going to the carnival and the rodeo." He hung up after recording his message and got dressed.

They left Joey's truck at the fire station and drove the few blocks to Weaver's Bakery. The morning rush was over, so they had the place to themselves.

"We haven't eaten here in months," Joey said as they followed their server to a corner booth.

"Looks the same," Wyatt observed. It was nice to enjoy the local spots once the tourists left town. The bakery slash cafe dated back to the forties or fifties and had a distinct grubbiness that somehow translated into a grandma's-kitchen-feel. The owner worked the cash register and baked pastries in the back. On the other hand, the cook resembled a prison break on the run. But since the guy could make a mean scramble, nobody bothered to check out his past.

Joey pushed his coffee mug around the yellowing Formica tabletop. "Know what you want?"

"Don't even have to look at the menu."

He grinned. "Yeah. Me neither."

They ate their eggs over easy on toast and hashbrowns with tabasco sauce before they spoke again. Wyatt wiped the final smudge of sun-yellow yoke from his plate with a corner of sourdough. "That hit the spot."

Joey leaned back and patted his belly. "I'm stuffed." He lifted his mug to his lips and eyed Wyatt over the rim. "But not too full for a cream cheese Danish." He chose one and slid the remaining pastry to the center of the table.

"What's up?"

Setting down his mug, Joey met Wyatt's question with a blush. "I need to apologize for my behavior lately." He tunneled his fingers through his hair. "I've been seeing a counselor."

Had he missed something in his best friend's life? "Are you okay?"

"I've been dealing with some stuff...a couple of medical calls I went on did weird things to my brain." He clenched his eyes closed and let out a breath before opening them. "Last night didn't help."

"The job takes a toll." Wyatt was no stranger to counseling. His third fatality accident in a month sent him spinning last year.

"I've been diagnosed with PTSD." Joey dropped Wyatt's gaze as if he were ashamed.

Wyatt leaned back against the booth. "Man." Guilt pricked him for avoiding his best friend. "If I'd have known—"

"My therapist says PTSD is common for firefighters." He pulled a slim paperback out of his jacket pocket. The cover was black with the Firefighter's Union logo featured on the front. "This will explain—and maybe help you someday."

A sudden thought shook Wyatt. "Bro, are you quitting the department?"

"No, but I'm taking some leave. I've been self-medicating, and I need to get sober." His mouth turned up into his usual disarming grin. "But hey, I'm learning techniques to deal with trauma." The grin faded, and his eyes filled. "So I can do my job without self-destructing."

The heavy breakfast weighed in Wyatt's belly like bricks. "What can I do, Joey?"

"Just don't make me worry about *you*."

"I'm fine."

Joey lifted a challenging brow. "We face tough situations every day in this line of work. Just promise you'll be aware."

"That's an easy promise, bro. You're one of the toughest guys I know, so if you're struggling, it could get me, too."

"Keep me updated on your girlfriend. I never got around to telling you how much I like her. She's different."

Wyatt let out a loud breath. "Yeah, Olivia's real sweet. But she's not officially my girlfriend. At least, not yet."

Joey's cocky smile made a reappearance. "Need advice from a pro?"

Wyatt laughed. "Thanks, but no thanks."

"Is she aware that behind your rugged good looks and uniform, you're actually a nerd like her?"

"Hey!"

"Sorry, I just mean, you know, she's not like the rest of the girls that hang around the crew." Joey held his hands up. "Not that that's a bad thing. Part of my therapy is avoiding those party girls."

Wyatt gave Joey a long, thoughtful look. "You might consider taking up bird watching. It's surprisingly therapeutic."

Joey wrinkled his nose. "By bird watching, do you mean duck hunting?"

Wyatt laughed. "Come on, let's take off. We have stairs to repair."

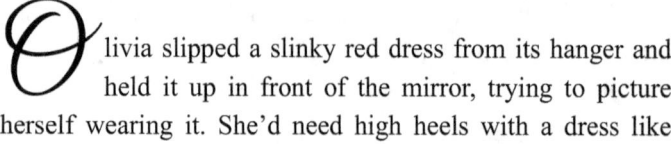

*O*livia slipped a slinky red dress from its hanger and held it up in front of the mirror, trying to picture herself wearing it. She'd need high heels with a dress like this, and since she never wore them, walking with dignity would be a problem.

Nina appeared in the mirror over Olivia's shoulder. "Ah… that might not be appropriate for the rodeo. I have serious questions about how you'll stay decent on the carnival rides."

"Right." Olivia hung the dress back on the rack.

Nina eyed Olivia. "You're about a size twenty-seven waist, right?" She hung a pair of dark wash jeans on a rack beside the mirror.

"You have a good eye."

"I should hope so, being a stylist and running the boutique since Shirley retired." Nina lifted a pretty blouse to the light of the chandelier hanging above the fitting area. "Too sheer," she pronounced.

The ivory loveseat and matching faux fur white rug on the floor made trying on clothing at Nina's boutique an event. The gold accents added another touch of luxury. Olivia usually bought her clothes from the same store where she bought groceries.

Nina tilted her head to indicate a drinks cart. "Mocktails. Help yourself. It's all part of the experience."

Olivia resembled a little brown bird more than ever, standing in such a plush, feminine atmosphere.

Nina turned around to capture Olivia's attention. "It's not meant to intimidate you. All this is meant to *inspire*."

Olivia gave her an unsure smile—the best she could do— and returned to the rack full of glittering dresses. She held up a green sequin number with a plunging neckline and turned to find Nina frowning at her.

"That's not you."

"I know, and that's the problem, remember? I'm trying to be someone else now."

Crossing her arms, Nina shook her head. "No, you're not.

If you don't like yourself, changing how you dress won't matter."

Olivia sighed. "I thought the point of this was to change me."

"Nope. The point is to uncover who you really are. Who have you been hiding underneath those sweaters and baggy pants? Finding out the wonderful parts of Olivia Lewis is what we're here to accomplish."

Settling the sequinned dress back on the rack, Olivia pinned her arms over her middle. "I haven't figured out who I am."

"I think the problem is more about permitting yourself to like who you are and less about reinventing yourself." Nina held her wrist up. "I promised to meet Sloan for an appointment with our financial firm down the block. I'm sorry, but I need to run." She waved to a striking, older woman at the other end of the boutique. "Gayle can help you, and I've already told her you can take anything you like home today. Your aunt's card is on file."

At Olivia's widening eyes, Nina winked.

"Millie anticipated you. She figured you'd come around sooner or later."

Nina's employee, Gayle, glided near, unnerving Olivia.

"She works on commission." Nina gave Olivia's shoulder a light tap. "See you at the carnival or rodeo."

"You're going to both?"

Nina shrugged. "Depending on how cranky my little person gets." She handed Olivia a pair of hoop earrings studded with gemstones. "These will go with everything. Bye now."

"Hello, darling." Gayle sparkled from her eyeshadow to the tips of her bejeweled fingernails. She wore a zebra print blouse, a layered gold chain necklace, and a taffeta skirt studded with roses made of ribbon.

Olivia's smile faltered. Gayle's gold shoes and dangling earrings caught the lighting from overhead. Olivia wasn't sure where to rest her eyes because the woman took up all the space around them. From her earrings to her orange lipstick, Gayle drew attention. The woman had to be pushing sixty, and the impression she gave suggested that fashion was more than her job. Still, Nina and Millie trusted her.

Gayle tossed a confident smile at Olivia and touched her earrings. "The chandelier style is very Ralph Lauren, summer line, but I think they'll be fabulous all year."

"Y-yes." Olivia knew nothing about Ralph Lauren's style but nodded as if she agreed.

"Let's get busy, doll. Nina says you're going for a casual but knock-out look for the carnival?"

"And the rodeo."

"Hmmm. I'm thinking rhinestones." She narrowed her eyes and motioned for Olivia to turn a circle. "Let me guess…" She tapped her lips. "There's a certain man in the picture, and you'd like to catch his eye."

That wasn't hard to guess. "More like a man who I'd like to keep around." Olivia glanced at Gayle's bare ring finger. Perhaps she wasn't the best choice for advice.

"Come with me, sweetness. I'm a woman of vision. Be prepared to dazzle your man."

Olivia kept up but just barely. Gayle was a dervish, snatching jewelry from hooks with one hand while disrobing mannequins with the other. She smiled over her shoulder as Olivia trailed her like a lost child.

"I'm thinking a leopard print blouse with black heels."

"I'm going to the rodeo."

"Right. Scratch the heels. You're no Nina." Gayle held up a pair of shiny leather trousers.

"Nina already chose a pair of jeans." Her mouth went dry when she spied Gayle, reaching for a very neon orange jacket. "I heard tan is in style this fall."

Gayle stopped and stared. "I think you mean camel, but that's for cashmere, darling." She rolled her eyes but chose a different jacket. "Leopard is a neutral staple for every stylish woman's closet."

Blinking, Olivia chose to keep her thoughts to herself, but her face must have spoken for her.

Gayle planted her hand on her hip and arched a brow. "Ask anybody."

What did Olivia know? Maybe Leopard was all the rage.

By the time Olivia walked out of the boutique, loaded with clothes, boots, makeup, and jewelry, she was dazed and confused. It could have been the cloud of Gayle's perfume fogging her brain. Or the baffling number of styles, colors, and fabrics Gayle had her trying on until she wanted to drop on the plush carpet. When Olivia wanted to call it quits, Gayle insisted on giving her a makeup tutorial that lasted over an hour.

Olivia trudged up Millie's front stairs and plunked down her bags, ready to collapse.

"It's about time. Your dinner is cold, and our movie is half over." Millie eyed the bags on the floor at Olivia's feet. She lifted her face, and a slow smile crinkled her eyes as she took in the layers of cosmetics. "Well, well. I see you've met Gayle."

Olivia hadn't recognized her face in the gilded mirror at the boutique. How would she recreate the look by herself tomorrow?

Millie lifted Olivia's chin with her finger and turned her

face to view Gayle's work from different angles. "Are you sure?"

Oh, Olivia was sure about this, alright. Shy Olivia, who stuttered when talking to strangers, who blushed, cringed, and let life go by without even trying?

That Olivia was gone forever.

# 12

## FOOLS FALL IN LOVE

The live band started their second set before Wyatt finally heard from Olivia. He glanced over at Joey after reading her text. "Olivia says she'll be here soon."

Joey glanced at his watch. "She's only three hours late." He rolled his eyes. "Women."

Joey stuck close to Wyatt, avoiding the beer garden near the rodeo where many of their friends were partying. "Here comes Hector." Wyatt jerked a thumb toward the burly medic.

Hector wore a sour expression.

Joey clapped him on the back. "What's wrong?"

"The kissing booth is passing out Hershey's Kisses." Hector shoved his hands in his pockets.

Joey howled.

Wyatt struggled to keep a straight face. "You thought some gorgeous woman would stand there and swap spit with strangers for a fundraiser?"

Hector toed the ground with his boot.

"I'll take that as a yes." Wyatt checked his phone for the thousandth time before meeting Hector's sad eyes. "You know, it's almost like you hoped for someone in particular to pucker up at the kissing booth."

Shrugging, Hector's gaze trailed away. "There is someone…but I'm too late."

"She's with someone else?" Joey craned his neck, trying to catch a glimpse of the kissing booth at the other end of the park.

"Looks that way," Hector said.

"Whoa. Guys…look at that." Joey pointed to a woman at the cotton candy stand.

There was something intriguing about her. She was slim but curvy and wore a pair of jeans that proved it. The jeans ended in calf-high leather boots. Her red blouse opened at the neck, showing creamy collarbones but not too much skin. The sun glinted on oversized gold hoops in delicate ears and a thick gold chain around her slender throat.

It was so hard not to look.

Hector and Joey stared, and Wyatt snuck another peek when her hair bounced in a shiny, long ponytail.

Olivia?

Olivia turned away from the vendor with a bag of cotton candy dangling from her fingers. Her lips were parted slightly as she met Wyatt's shocked gaze. A familiar fringe of bangs over dark, saucer eyes made Wyatt blink. It couldn't be. But when her cheeks bunched in a shy smile and their eyes tangled…

Joey's eyebrows shot up, and he whistled. "Is that?"

"I think so," Hector said.

"Olivia?" Wyatt rubbed his eyes.

"Dude…" Joey elbowed Wyatt.

"I know."

Olivia blushed but then raised her chin and waved before sliding the bag of candy inside her purse.

Hector grabbed his backpack. "Let's take a walk, Joey."

Wyatt barely registered his friends' absence as Olivia walked toward him sans glasses and all big eyes and rosy lips. The smile she landed on him stole Wyatt's breath. Her approach was achingly slow, but his heart raced as she strolled closer.

"Liv?" His voice cracked, tongue fused to the inside of his mouth.

She paused, close enough to touch now, but Wyatt was disarmed, unsure if he should. But then Olivia reached out, her hands grazing his forearms as she slipped her arms around his neck. Her brown eyes lifted and scanned his. "Hello, Wyatt." Her voice was different...husky.

Wyatt swallowed.

The scent of her, the pressure of her body pressed to his, sent his heart flapping inside his chest like a bird caught in a cage. But it was all...wrong.

His Olivia wasn't a seductress. His Olivia was shy and sweet and—

"Sorry, I'm late."

He caught his breath when her words melted warm in his ear.

She pulled away just enough to give him a bold glance. He'd never seen her without glasses. Dark brown globes framed with long lashes that swept her cheeks held him frozen, unable to think straight—only feel.

"Well?" A lazy smile pulled at her lips. "What do you think?"

He wanted to say he thought she was prettier without all that makeup, but he wasn't stupid.

She waited for a response, but Wyatt's mouth was dry as sand. It took a few tries to get any words out. "I-I didn't recognize you."

Olivia unclasped her hands from the back of his neck and slid them down to rest on his chest. "Good," she said in a husky tone.

"Good?" He sputtered.

With a coy smile, Olivia slanted her eyes at him. "The old Olivia is gone. You don't have to be embarrassed to be seen with me now." She gave a playful shrug and struck a pose.

Wyatt's initial surprise and attraction drained to disappointment. "But, I liked you the way you were."

They stared at each other for a long time before Wyatt could be sure he'd said the words out loud. Maybe he was stupid after all.

Olivia's smile melted, and splotchy red spots stained her throat and face.

Wyatt cupped her face in his hands. "Liv, I'm crazy about you. Just the way I met you. I liked you then. I like you now." He took a breath. "In fact, I more than like you."

But Olivia wasn't listening to him. Her eyes were pools of hurt, and her mouth twisted in a vulnerable frown. She was going to cry.

"Oh, Liv. I didn't mean to hurt your feelings, I just—"

Before he could reassure her, she spun around, dodged his hands, and fled.

"Olivia, wait!"

But she didn't, and he wasn't sure if chasing her in a public place would result in an emotional disaster

*O*livia had never felt so ridiculous, and there'd been plenty of opportunities. But trying too hard for Wyatt and getting rejected in front of God and the whole town? That took the prize.

She headed as fast as her legs would move to the safety of her favorite bench on the waterfront, far enough from the crowded carnival that she would escape any more humiliation but close enough that she might not feel lonely.

She stuffed a handful of purple cotton candy into her mouth and swallowed around the fist-sized lump in her throat.

She wasn't going to cry.

She refused to cry.

She was crying.

Wiping her eyes on the hem of her silk blouse, she avoided eye contact with an attractive couple walking along with their fingers twined together. The sun shone on them from between the leaves of the trees over the path, and their radiant faces glowed as they stared into one another's eyes.

She was so alone.

Unzipping the purse she'd bought with Gayle's persuasion from the Desert Rose boutique, she opened her new compact and cringed. Okay, maybe she'd overdone the makeover. She rubbed at ruby lips that made her resemble a child playing dress-up. Turning her face to view each side, her heart sank at the twin bright red stains on her cheeks. The blush didn't suit her at all, but in her defense, the bathroom lighting had been soft and misleading at Millie's. It was plain that she required some practice putting on makeup.

She blinked away tears of self-pity. At least she'd mastered her contact lenses. That had been a hassle but worth the trouble, not worrying about smudged glasses slipping down her nose all the time. Snapping the clasp on the little gold makeup mirror, she stuffed it back into her purse and set the bag aside. Time to process the mess she'd made of her sweet relationship with Wyatt.

Closing her eyes, she replayed getting dressed, applying and reapplying makeup before she flounced like a floozy through the park.

She cringed as she recalled the looks on Wyatt's friends' faces. She'd not only made a fool of herself but Wyatt too. She held a hand over her stomach and tried to calm her rapid breathing. How could she be so stupid? The guys laughed at women who threw themselves at the fire crew. Wyatt avoided them, and she'd just spent a fortune to look the part--not to mention acting the part--in front of his friends.

She should have waited for Nina to help with the makeover instead of taking Gayle's advice.

Olivia groaned and covered her face with her hands. She was very likely smearing lipstick and mascara all over herself, but she wanted to hide her shame somewhere. No convenient sinkhole appeared.

A gentle breeze came in off the water, lifting Olivia's hair away from her hot forehead. She parted her hands to inhale the sweet scent of fall leaves. She stilled, soaking in the tranquility surrounding her like comforting arms. It had grown quiet in the park aside from birdsong. But a message floated to her silently, penetrating her wounds with words of acceptance and belonging. She sensed power, love, and kindness that could only be the Lord there with her, bathing her injured heart with grace. Rather than a reprimand for her pride and insecurity, He was singing love songs to her through the birds and the wind and the lapping of the waves on the lakeshore.

Olivia began to weep again. Not tears of shame this time,

but of gratitude. She'd lost her way—let her identity get knotted up with her appearance rather than Christ's love.

After a while, Olivia's breathing calmed. She sat with her eyes closed and her body still, fingers limp on her thighs.

Wyatt said he liked her—that he more than liked her.

Surely, he could forgive her for her foolish behavior. She'd wanted attention, and boy, had she gotten it. How long would Hector and Joey retell the story at the Rose & Thorn? She'd gotten demoralized today but blessed, too. She'd shared an intimate time with the Lord. God had turned her foolishness into an opportunity for inner growth. No matter what Wyatt chose to do because of the embarrassing incident, she had that.

Olivia stood and shook out her stiff limbs. The skin of her face was tight—probably puffy from crying—and her vision fuzzy. In the future, she'd think twice before crying while wearing contact lenses. She took her time walking home and let herself in the back door. She climbed the stairs to use the mirror with stronger lighting this time and took stock of her appearance.

What had she been thinking?

After scrubbing her face clean, she flipped the switch and crept down the hall to her room. The blouse was unsuitable for a carnival, but she liked it for a future wine tasting or a play. She tossed it over a chair to take to the dry cleaners and pulled on her olive green sweater instead. It went well with her new boots. The gold jewelry made her dark eyes appear to have hints of amber, so she'd keep the earrings and necklace.

Olivia scrounged through her toiletry bag. A light touch of pink lipstick, rather than the bright red, made her feel like herself, only prettier.

It was time to return to the carnival.

If Wyatt avoided her she would accept his decision. She squared her shoulders. Olivia intended to enjoy the festivities with Millie and her Birding Betty friends. Slipping her new crossbody bag over her head, she walked out the front door with her chin up.

When Olivia reached the park entrance, she showed the stamp on her hand to the attendant to show she'd already paid. To her despair, she'd missed the rodeo completely. Disappointed, her resolve wilted a bit. Especially when she caught the scent of sweet and pungent sweat from a line of horses tied to horse trailers in a field on her way to find her friends. The tired beasts rested, heads down and eyes closed behind a white fence that separated the carnival crowd from the rodeo.

The sign for the Hooked On Ewe Knitting Club was just ahead of her when her cell phone buzzed with a text from Millie.

Need you at the shop stall ASAP

*M*illie probably wanted Olivia to take her turn demonstrating knitting stitches for carnival-goers. Making her way past the kettle corn vendor, the allure of butter, salt, and burned sugar proved too much. She bought a bag for later and headed for Millie's stall.

"There you are." Millie wasn't fast but darted her arm out and caught Olivia. "Wyatt and I have been searching for you."

"Wyatt?" His name shot out of her throat just as her stomach dropped to her feet.

She kept an iron grip on Olivia's arm and propelled her to the park's edge. "Come on."

Olivia dug her feet in the soft grass and refused to go further when she caught sight of the big red fire engine. Millie pulled. Olivia shook her head, but Millie waved to someone behind her. Olivia turned to find a crowd of familiar faces.

The knitting club— AKA the Meddling Mamas—and Olivia's knitting students, along with most of the Birding Betties. Nina and Sloan held hands and smiled. A group of firefighters with their ever-present groupies clustered near the edge of the grass like they were waiting for a show to start.

Olivia's chest tightened.

The fire engine's lights began to flash, and a loud noise from the speaker on top of the rig made Olivia jump.

Wyatt's face appeared in the driver's window, wearing a cheesy smile. He held the intercom to his mouth and tested it over the engine's speaker system. "Testing, testing." Loud and clear. "Olivia Lewis, please come to the front of the crowd."

Olivia's heart tried to shoot out of her rib cage. She stepped back, ready to run. What was Wyatt doing?

Wyatt shoved open the door and jumped down in full bunker gear, landing on the blacktop in heavy black boots. He brandished the intercom high, the spiral cord stretched taught. He motioned for Olivia to come to him.

Olivia scanned the group, skin itching because everyone's gaze was on her, waiting for her reaction.

Her body prepared to vault over anything in her way, yet trust in the wonderful man she'd come to know so well smothered the panic.

She'd embarrassed herself for him, and now he was doing the same for her. He kept her guessing, but not about his character. Wyatt was too kind to embarrass her. He'd never do something to hurt her, especially in front of all these people.

She threw her shoulders back and walked toward him.

Wyatt winked at the crowd. Aside from the girls with their phones out, everyone clapped. Someone hooted. When Olivia stood in front of him, Wyatt held his hand out. He showed her a piece of paper that fluttered from his fingers. "Olivia Lewis, I'm with the Wild Rose Fire Department. This is an official citation."

She blinked.

He held the paper closer.

She cleared her throat. "A citation? For what?"

His face gave her no clues.

"For being too hot." He handed the paper to Olivia. "Just the way you are."

Heat rose from her face in waves, and Olivia couldn't decide whether to smack Wyatt or kiss him.

But he wasn't finished. "I'm crazy about you. I love everything about you." He brought his fingers to his lips and whistled over his shoulder. "I was hooked the first day I met you."

Steve jumped out of the back of the engine and trotted to Olivia with wilted, slobbery flowers in his mouth. He dropped them at her feet and sat. He wore the sweater Olivia knitted for him. Olivia sniffed back emotion.

Everyone faded but Wyatt. Olivia crouched down to retrieve the bouquet, patted Steve, and pressed the bouquet to her heart. Wyatt tossed the intercom through the fire engine window and opened his arms to her. She rushed to him, melting into his chest.

He kissed the top of her head. "Will you be my girl-friend?" This time, the words weren't on the loudspeaker. He whispered them into her ear with a warm breath that sent shivers down her spine.

They crushed the flowers between them, releasing their sweet scent. The fragrance reminded what happened when the Lord met her at the bench. Olivia wrapped her arms around Wyatt's waist and buried her face in the hollow space under his collarbone. Her answer was muffled but only meant for Wyatt's ears anyway. "Yes!"

She lifted her face for the kiss she'd wanted for so long but had been too shy to claim. Wyatt gazed down at her with tenderness and turned their bodies so his back was to the crowd, shielding Olivia. He brushed his thumb over her bottom lip, causing her pulse to jump, before he angled his head toward hers and pressed his lips against her mouth.

Olivia rose on tiptoes, deepening their kiss. Surely, the way her blood whistled through her ears meant the angels were singing. Having Wyatt's strong arms around her and his lips hungry on hers was a taste of heaven.

She didn't even care that they were surrounded by cheering, clapping people watching them kiss.

## 13

---

# EPILOGUE
## SUNNY DAYS

*O*livia shifted her bag to the other hand and signed the guest book at the front desk of Sunny Days Retirement Home.

The receptionist gave her a bright smile. "So glad to have you back, Olivia. Mr. Swensen looks forward to your weekly visits."

"So do I, Mrs. Kip."

She took her time walking to room seventeen, stopping to greet Gertrude and Amelia, playing cards as usual in the recreation room. These two had become like surrogate grandmothers to Olivia, sharing their wisdom and life experiences. Afterward, she popped in to check in on Mrs. Schweitzer, one of the Birding Betties.

Mr. Swensen moved into the home after a tumble down his basement stairs, surprising them all with how well he'd settled in. His old friend Pappy Rosmund lived here, and that helped. Olivia became acquainted with the man's granddaughter, Ruthie, who visited every week. She was a conspirator of Millie's, one of the knitting club members notorious for matchmaking.

Olivia couldn't be mad at the Meddling Mammas. After all, they'd helped her find the man of her dreams.

"There you are." Mr. Swensen guided his wheelchair from the doorway of his room into the hall. "I hope you're hungry. That aunt of yours brought more cookies yesterday." The gruff old dear pointed to the bag swinging from her hand. "Whatcha got?" He sniffed the air, trying to scent for tacos, which he often requested but must have forgotten to do today.

Olivia pulled out a blue beanie she knitted for her new friend. "You complained about your head getting cold, so I thought this might help keep you warm." The beanie was a symbol of their friendship, a tangible expression of her care for him.

"So I did. You're a brilliant girl, you know that?" He took the hat from her and snugged it down over his head. "Perfect fit," he declared. His shirt buttons were misaligned, and his trousers unzipped, but he seemed in good spirits even if he was a little unkempt.

"You shaved."

"You noticed."

She hid her smile. "It's freezing outside today, so how about we visit on the sofa in front of the fireplace in the dayroom?"

His mouth turned down. He grumbled about being cooped up but started rolling his wheelchair down the hall anyway.

"Hey, I can't keep up." She stopped to give Myrtle Jenkins a library book in room nine.

"You're such a blessing, dear." Myrtle planted a kiss on Olivia's cheek.

Olivia returned the kiss. Myrtle's velvety-soft cheek smelled like face powder—which Olivia had come to think of as comforting. "Mrs. Jenkins, you're the blessing."

"Hey, you comin' or what?" Mr. Swensen grumped from his spot near the fireplace. He didn't like sharing Olivia.

Myrtle rolled her eyes, and they laughed.

"On my way," Olivia called. He was always eager for the new photos of the sheep on her phone and to get news about the farm.

Settling her purse on the floor, she tugged off her gloves and held them to the fire. "Did the cook's Christmas dinner meet your expectations?"

"It certainly did. I haven't had a meal that fine since…" He glanced up at the ceiling as if a calendar was up there. "Well, I don't know when." He rolled closer to the sofa, set the brakes, flipped up the pedals, and then eased his creaky body to land beside her. He folded his hands over his belly, and his lips turned up.

"I'm happy to hear that." She offered him a lap blanket from the basket near the fire. The knitting club kept it stocked.

"How about you? Did you have a pleasant visit with your folks?" He spread the quilt over his thin legs.

"It was nice to finally introduce my parents to Wyatt and his family. I think Millie enjoyed having her house full for a week." She grinned. "But probably just as glad when everyone cleared out."

Mr. Swensen plucked at his long eyebrows and glanced at her bag. "I'm sure Millicent is a bit lonely since you moved to the farm."

That was Olivia's cue. She unzipped her purse and dug her phone out to show him the newest lamb. "Millie and I still have our popcorn and movie nights. We just schedule around Wyatt's shifts." She swiped the screen to open the photos. "Look at Bernice's little ewe lamb. Isn't she adorable? She's tiny, but Wyatt looked her over and said she's fine."

"She's nursing on both sides and playing with Joyce's lamb?" Mr. Swensen was invested in the flock, even from his retirement home, and asked about each sheep by name.

"Joyce's lamb is rambunctious." Olivia chuckled. "I'm still shocked that any of the girls were bred."

He snorted. "They were left to their own devices too often when I was tryin' to go it alone. Where there's a will, there's a way."

Olivia chuckled. "I suppose so, but Wyatt helped me reinforce the ram's pen, so surprise babies will be less likely."

"Let me see those lambs again, eh?" He leaned over.

Olivia loved watching the lambs and captured several videos for him every week.

Ten minutes later, he'd seen every photo and video twice, and his eyes drooped.

Olivia touched his arm. "I came a bit later than usual today, sorry. You must be tired out."

He lifted his eyes to her, and she caught her breath as tears pooled in them.

"What is it?"

He clapped his huge hand over hers, liver spots showing his age and calloused fingers his life-long industry. "I'm thankful for you. I stayed in my house too long because I was afraid of what would happen to my critters. Without any family around… they'd just be sold at auction."

Olivia swallowed the emotion choking her at seeing her elderly friend in tears. "That's an unbearable thought."

Taking away his overlarge hand, he swiped at his eyes with the back of it. "Intolerable. But now you're there. You love the girls as much as I do, and that's an answer to prayer, I tell ya."

"I'm so grateful you trusted me. Buying your farm and flock is a dream come true for me."

They sat in silence for a while, soaking in God's goodness at allowing their paths to cross, and then Olivia tapped Mr. Swensen's leg. "I forgot to tell you that last weekend, a stray cat showed up, and since I needed a mouser—and I felt sorry for her—I've been feeding her. I even put a little basket on the porch with a blanket inside."

"A cat, you say?" His wooly eyebrows gathered in disapproval.

Olivia nodded, unperturbed. "On the second night, she cried and cried at the door until I finally let her inside."

"What will Steve think about a cat in the house?" He frowned.

"He likes cats, and anyway, he doesn't live on the farm yet." She scrolled her photo app. "I think she needed a safe place to have her babies."

"What? Kittens?" The gruff expression melted into a soft-eyed smile. "Who doesn't like kittens, I ask you?"

"I love them. We have four gray tabbies and an orange one. Their little mewing is so sweet."

"Wyatt's seen them?"

"I called him when she went into labor. You know Wyatt, he came right over to help."

Mr. Swensen's loud guffaw startled a resident nodding in a chair across the hall. "A firefighter delivering kittens. Oh, that's rich." He slapped his thigh.

"I was grateful for his help." Olivia has grown used to his rough edges. "Anyway, I'll start looking for homes, so they have families waiting for them when they're old enough."

"Good." He pointed at Olivia's hand. "Now, about that big rock on your finger? You haven't said a word about it."

Olivia lifted her ring finger and let the diamond sparkle in the warm fire's glow.

"You gonna spill the tea?"

No matter how hard she tried, she couldn't have stopped the smile from splitting her face. "Wyatt asked me to marry him on Christmas Eve."

"You got married, and you didn't invite me?" Mr. Swensen's tone suggested insult.

Olivia met his eyes. "Heavens, no, he only asked me. We set a date in May," she went on to clear up the misunderstanding. "I promise you'll be invited to the ceremony."

Mr. Swensen harumphed. "Speak of the devil."

"Hi guys, sorry I'm late, but Bible study ran long." Wyatt carried a box from Weaver's Bakery under one arm. He stooped to drop a kiss on Olivia's forehead. "I take it you heard the news?" he questioned Mr. Swensen.

"Hearty congratulations are in order. You picked yourself a beauty." Mr. Swensen held out his hand.

"I'm aware of my good fortune, trust me." Wyatt laughed and shook the offered hand.

"Sit down, son. Tell me how you netted this little fish here. I never found a wife, you know. I was like a fox without a tail."

At Olivia's questioning brow and Wyatt's shrug, Mr. Swensen coughed. "Nothing fancy to draw the female eye."

"Oh." Olivia wasn't sure how to respond.

Wyatt saved her. "Olivia wants to hold the reception at the farm." He sat beside her and draped his arm over her shoulder.

Mr. Swensen brightened. "Do tell."

"My family and a few friends are helping me with the bigger jobs and Olivia's planting flower bulbs. The farm will look like a proper wedding venue when we finish. I'll make sure you get a trip out to the farm to see for yourself."

With misty eyes, Mr. Swensen nodded. "Thank you. I started feelin' pretty lonely until you came along to check on me all those months ago."

Wyatt clasped his elder's forearm. "You've been a huge blessing to my girl and me. Thank you for making her so happy."

"You won't mind living on the farm and helpin' Olivia tend the sheep?"

"Nothing I'd love more. Liv loves those sheep, and I love her."

Nodding approval, Mr. Swensen belched quietly. "I imagine she'll take over Hooked On Ewe when Millicent retires. Have you thought about that possibility?"

"I can handle the shop and the farm," Olivia piped up.

Wyatt patted Olivia's leg. "Hooked On Ewe has been around since before I was born. We'll figure things out when and *if* we're faced with the decision." He squeezed Olivia's shoulder. "Whatever we do, we'll do it together."

Olivia met Wyatt's eyes and leaned in to rest her head on his shoulder. She lifted her hand to admire her ring. "I have a lot going for me since I met you." She'd never dreamed she could be so happy, and the future would only get better with a man like Wyatt Simms.

*The End*

# HOW TO HELP…

*If you enjoyed this book, I'd appreciate it so much if you would gift me with a short review. They help so much!*

Thank you,
Dalyn

Leave A Review

# ABOUT THE AUTHOR

Dalyn Weller writes inspirational, small-town romance novels with a bit of wit and a pinch of humor.

She lives on a horse ranch surrounded by apple orchards and cattle in Washington State with her husband and their youngest son.

Two beautiful horses, three dogs, a flock of chickens, three retired dairy goats, and a few barn cats make their home on the ranch.

Dalyn enjoys her family, horses, gardening, morning mocha cappuccinos, and afternoon tea. She writes from a cozy office overlooking the barn.

You can find Dalyn and the critters on her social media accounts.

Be sure to sign up for her newsletter: Writing from the Ranch:

http://gem.godaddy.com/signups/
b8a3c9a022534072b2e6b69e142cc966/join

Scan for newsletter

facebook.com/DalynWellerAuthor

instagram.com/dalynweller

goodreads.com/DalynWeller

bookbub.com/authors/dalyn-weller

pinterest.com/dalynweller

# ALSO BY DALYN WELLER

The Rancher's Surprise Second Chance

Fashioned For Love

Love Happens At Sweetheart Farm

available at
amazon

AUTUMN IN WILD ROSE RIDGE SERIES

# Kyle's
# Autumn
# Blaze

## LINDA JO REED

# EXCERPT: KYLE'S AUTUMN BLAZE
## PROLOGUE

### LINDA JO REED

*M*argaret Walcott tapped her empty knitting
needle against her teeth while lost in thought.
There was just no end to the work for the Hooked On Ewe
Knitting Club. No, no, it had nothing to do with turning out
knitted goods, though some of the gals did take that task seri-
ously. But most of the women enjoyed being together to
gossip and more important, to make matches for their
offspring.

So far, Margaret's children had been cooperative. Even
when they didn't know they were being pushed into a match.
And even when they were being pushed *away* from a match,
which was the case with Kellie and Raul. But, Margaret had
to admit, that was a fine pairing even if she'd opposed it at
the start.

"What's got you in the doldrums today, Margaret?" Ellen
Sutherland eyed her as she clicked her needles. Ellen was one
who could knit. Margaret supposed it was all the time she
spent during her cancer treatment last year that gave her the

time to learn. Margaret was sure that Ellen had never picked up a pair of knitting needles before that.

"I'm thinking about my children."

"But that should make you happy. You've had some great success at getting them paired off." Miriam Hanford pointed out.

Margaret smoothed back her already tightly coiffed white-blond hair and ran a hand across the chignon on her neck, careful not to catch her rings in her "do." Satisfied that every hair was in place, she dropped her hand to finger the yarn and needles in her lap.

"Yes, of course I am pleased. But now my eldest son, Kyle, poses a problem. I just know he is going to resist every step of the way."

"Well, his wife, Amber, was such a lovely girl. It's no wonder he has mourned her passing so long," Diana Alexander, Margaret's sister said. "I remember some good talks we used to have."

"She was," Margaret affirmed. "But he has lived in his own rose tower for years now and it's time he got out there again."

"Hmm," the ladies murmured their own concerns for their offspring, but Margaret tuned them out.

Everyone went through grief when they lost someone, but Kyle had carried it to an extreme. It was time for him to get out among the living. His roses weren't going anywhere. Heaven knew, Margaret's husband Gerald was probably tending them from heaven. Kyle could leave Rose Cliff Gardens now and then.

But how to make that happen?

Margaret knew just the right woman for him. In fact, he was already interested but he didn't yet know it. All it would take was a little *push*. All the help Margaret would need for that little operation surrounded her. She looked around the room at her friends.

Now just might be the time to start the campaign.

# *C*hapter One

*A*lene Peterson struggled as she dragged the tall Ficus plant over by the front door of Roses & Blooms. The door swung open and yanked her off balance and the plant began to tip. Alene grabbed for it but her fist met air and she felt herself overbalancing.

"Whoa! Watch it there!" Strong arms stopped her fall.

"Kyle Walcott, you just happened to walk in now?" Alene laughed as she met the amused brown eyes towering over her. They softened as he held her, and awareness tingled through her body.

"What's happened? I heard a crash," Bette Noone, owner of Roses & Blooms, came rushing from the back room with assistant and delivery driver, Kris Rool, behind her. Bette's faded red hair stuck out from her head as looked around the shop quickly before her glance passed between Kyle and Alene in their compromising position in front of the front door.

Kris moved toward the fallen plant and Bette put her hands on her hips.

"What is this?" She demanded with a laugh.

Kris stifled a smile and reached for the foliage.

Kyle lifted Alene and set her on her feet. He pushed back

the cowboy hat that had slid toward his face, then bent to help Kris pick up the plant and clear the entrance.

"It looks like my arrival was timely this morning," he chuckled as he righted the plant. His brows rose as he turned Alene's way.

"Over there," she pointed and they rustled the plant into its new spot.

"Well, at least no one is hurt," Bette heaved a sigh of relief.

Alene's gaze caught Kyle's. She mouthed "thank you" and he nodded.

"Bette, where do you want your delivery to go?" Kyle's attention went to Bette and her arms flew as she gave him directions for the plant boxes. Kyle disappeared out the front door and down the steps to his van to pull out a few more bare root roses, small houseplants, and Alene noticed he had a few fall flowers, several colors of chrysanthemums, in pots for them this time.

"I'd like to start the morning in the arms of a handsome man, you lucky girl," Kris giggled and waved her fingers at Alene as she returned to the back room to await Kyle's delivery.

Alene's breath whooshed as she watched him go. She'd ignored Kris' comment, but when she turned around to continue her pre-opening tasks, she caught Bette's speculative look.

"What?"

"That plant was heavy. Why didn't you holler for help?"

"Just trying to save you time. There's a lot to do in the mornings."

"Uh huh. I suppose that's one way to get a man's attention." Bette grinned.

"I wasn't trying to get Kyle's attention, for heaven's sake.

We're friends. I don't think of him that way. Besides, he's my sister's uncle."

"But no relation to you."

"Just stop it, Bette."

"Just saying. Oh, thanks, Kyle. Just follow me. Although it's not like you haven't been delivering plants here for years." Bette winked at Alene as Kyle followed her with the boxes.

Alene muttered as she picked up a flowering shrub to set on the steps outside the front door and turned to fetch another one, nearly running into Kyle again.

"We have to stop meeting this way," he said.

Alene rolled her eyes. "Right."

He chuckled and sprinted down the steps for the next armload of boxes.

Alene darted inside for another colorful bush and waited for Kyle to stride across the shop before she headed outside again. Alene finally stepped back from the entrance to the shop to view her handiwork. It had to be inviting to draw customers.

*What is wrong with me?* This sudden shyness around Kyle confused her. She'd known him for a year or so, seen him in family situations, thanks to her sister Kellie. And now she saw him in some kind of new—and mystifying—light. What was this? Hadn't her experience with Scott been enough?

As if her thoughts conjured up Kyle, his form appeared at the doorway, backlit by the lights of the shop. In the early morning atmosphere, Alene heard birds singing and shook her head. *Like some kind of cheap movie.*

Kyle sprinted down the steps, headed to his van and shut the back doors.

"You have a good day, Alene. I'll see you soon. Say hi to

my niece when you see her," he saluted her, went around the van and climbed in.

She watched him drive slowly up the street and turn the corner.

Staring after him, her vision finally took in the people rushing in and out of Magic Beans next door and Rosehips Tea and Books across the street. People picking up their morning coffee before work.

Alene's gaze took in The Ridge Hotel, standing at the end Main Street. Alene and Kris would need to go up there later in the morning. That order was already stored in a refrigerated unit until they could get there later this morning to make flower arrangements. A long standing agreement between Bette, Ned and Bonne Mason, her relatives who owned the hotel, assured that giant cut flowers would be delivered to the hotel weekly to be stored there until she could get there to make the magnificent displays set around the lobby. That now fell to Alene. She loved creating them. She only hoped she could keep up the reputation that Bette had built for magnificent floral displays.

Kyle had long since disappeared and here she stood. She shook herself and scrambled back up the steps into the shop, suddenly breathless.

*Really, Alene?*

Framed in the doorway, Alene caught a reflection of light caught in the windows of Rosehips Tea and Books. She rushed back out into the street to stare at the steeple of Rosehill Community Church as it pointed skyward on the hill above the town behind the flower shop. The first sunrays of the day lit the cross. Alene's favorite moment. Every morning, she tried to be in a position to watch it. It felt like God's blessing for the day.

The scent of the South Thorn River, a couple streets over

from Roses & Blooms, wafted by her senses. And though she couldn't see Wild Rose Lake from here, she knew it lay just beyond the hotel.

She loved the hush that preceded the day. Just as the sky lightened.

*Thank you, God, for this new day.*

She had to get to the back room to help Bette and Kris with floral arrangements and orders. She started to shut the door but couldn't stop herself from one more glance up the street in case she could see where Kyle had stopped.

\*\*\*

A prickling at the back of his neck suggested to Kyle that Alene's eyes were still following him. He glanced at the side mirror to see her still standing in the street. He nearly hit the curb before returning his attention to the windshield. He couldn't help looking again, this time out of the other side mirror as he turned the corner. He saw Alene run up the shop steps and disappear.

He let out a breath he hadn't realized he'd been holding. Maybe he should have sent Ted out on deliveries today. He didn't give himself time to wonder why.

Rose Cliff Gardens had the city contract for the hanging baskets that lined the streets of Wild Rose Ridge. He, or whoever did deliveries on any day, checked on them to make sure they stayed fresh. As he jumped out of the refrigerated van, he noticed the sun had risen over the eastern mountains. He walked to the front of the vehicle to see if the cross was shining above the church on the hill. He stood for a moment watching the gilding on the cross against the indigo sky. The blue lightened behind the cross and the glory faded as the sun rose higher. Only God could arrange something so tran-scendent.

Kyle took his time checking and watering baskets. It was

getting late in the season and soon they'll be pulling in all the baskets hanging on the lampposts. It'll be time to change seasons. He could hardly believe that summer was coming to an end and the sun already slanted in its autumn glow. At least the heat wasn't as hot as the direct sun of summer. He liked the warm glow of autumn.

His thoughts lazily slid toward who might do the hotel floral arrangements once Bette retired from Roses & Blooms. She had owned that business and done the flowers for the hotel for nearly forty years. He wondered if Alene would be doing them from now on.

He shook his head. Why did he even have that thought? He'd never given any thoughts to who would handle the hotel flowers before.

He finished with the hanging baskets as the morning waned. Coffee was calling his name. His habit was to stop at Magic Beans Coffee Shop before doing his New Town route. But today, he merely glanced in the direction of Magic Beans as he kept the van on Rose Ridge Boulevard toward New Town. He would get coffee in New Town.

*Come on, Walcott, be honest. You are avoiding Alene Peterson.* Roses & Blooms was next door to Magic Beans.

Kyle ran a hand across his forehead. *Get a grip, man.*

He glanced at the lake as he drove. The sun sparkled on the water. He loved the mornings. A few fishing boats had been out there earlier on his trip into The Ridge, but now some sailboats drifted. More cars were on the road and people strode on foot between the park and town.

He left Wild Rose Ridge behind and traveled the short distance to New Town. He glanced in his rearview mirror. Not for traffic, but because he'd left Roses & Blooms back there. Well, he'd left Alene Peterson back there.

Right.

Kyle put her out of his mind as he finished his supply route. No hanging baskets charmed the streets in New Town. Too bad. It could use some kind of beautification project to offset the asphalt and concrete. Oh well, not his problem. Normally, doing his job was second nature. He'd been doing this for years. However, today he'd had to fight to keep his mind on his work.

By lunch time he was heading home to Rose Cliff Gardens at Walcott Orchards. His stomach growled. After lunch, he couldn't wait to get out in the gardens. He knew who he was there. He had purpose there. And he could handle the surprises there. Mostly.

What had happened back at Roses & Blooms? He hadn't held a woman in his arms since—since Amber died. He never intended to. But when Alene had dropped into his arms that morning, the feel of her brought back feelings he'd never thought to feel again.

# WILD ROSE RIDGE SERIES

If you would like to read more of Linda Jo Reed's novella or any of the other books in the Wild Rose Ridge series, you can find them on Amazon.

**Available in print, ebook, and Kindle Unlimited.**